WHAT HAPPENED AT
SUNRISE GARDENS

WHAT HAPPENED AT SUNRISE GARDENS

Nate Southard

CEMETERY DANCE PUBLICATIONS

Baltimore

❖ 2024 ❖

Cemetery Dance Publications
132B Industry Lane, Unit #7
Forest Hill, MD 21050

www.cemeterydance.com

Will you follow me? Will you walk hand in hand with God until the end of your days?

Yes, Father!

Do you believe in Him, and do you believe in me?

Yes, Father!

Cast out the evil! Cast out the wicked! This world is a rotten world, and it does not deserve the likes of our purity! We came here—we came here as one! As a community! The world out there, they shun us! They despise us because we believe in equality! And freedom! We believe in the righteous idea that men and women, black and white, all deserve happiness, that we all deserve a good life!

Amen!

Hate! Hate is what fuels that wicked world! They hate us for our freedom and for the love we feel as a community. They hate us for living in a way they never will. More than anything, they hate us for breaking free of the chains of their hatred. We have seen the light of equality, and they despise us for doing what they could not!

Amen!

One day they will come for us. They will seek to eradicate our community and all we have built. Will we let them?

No!

Will we let them place us back in chains?

No!

Will we let them raze Sunrise Gardens to the ground? Let them put our children in slavery? Will we stand by and give those who would do us harm the satisfaction of a victory for evil and tyranny and injustice?

No!

Then I ask you, brothers and sisters—I ask you, my children—prove it to me. Come. Step forward. Drink.

"CHILDREN. LINE UP. WE'VE practiced this. You know your order."

Most of the kids did as they were told, falling into a single file column at the classroom door. Three of the boys either took their time or seemed to ignore her altogether. Again, the call to assembly came, and Elizabeth ground her teeth before speaking. She adored the kids, but sometimes…

She breathed deep and forced herself calm. Patience was a virtue, and she knew hers had worn thin. The previous night's tribunal and drill had gone so late. By her best guess, she'd received two hours of sleep, maybe a little more. That meant the children had received about the same. No wonder they were so unruly today. Perhaps she could have a talk with Reverend Shaw. After such a late night, surely they deserved a morning off from their lessons.

Watching them run around, moving slowly toward the classroom's door, she wondered why they needed another tribunal so soon.

"Micah! Sam! Reggie! Get in line, now." Her voice bit, more commanding than she thought her twenty years should allow.

Reverend Shaw had repeatedly told everyone how powerful they were, though. Commanders. Leaders. Teachers. It's how they became such a strong community. Considering this, she straightened her back and smiled the slightest bit. No meek little waif here, sir. Even exhaustion couldn't keep her from her duties.

Two of the boys fell into line, their faces guilty. Shuffling, the children waited, ready to go.

Reggie remained in the classroom's far corner. A book sat in his lap, and he turned the pages casually, taking in the pictures. If he heard the airhorn's short-short-long blasts, he ignored them. *Oh, Reg,* she thought. *What would a day be without a trial from you?*

Elizabeth stretched out the fingers of her right hand and clenched them into a fist a few times. The jungle humidity left her hand feeling sore some days. Embarrassed by the lingering injury, she crouched beside the boy. She spent a second studying the cartoon bears cavorting across the pages, then she placed a single hand on the center of his back. "Reggie, it's time to go. You hear it, right?"

"Yeah."

"So we need to go, right?"

"I don't want to. Don't want to do it again."

A long breath slipped past her teeth. "I know we've been practicing a lot lately, but you know why we practice, don't you?"

"So we get better."

"That's right. So we get better, until we're the best we can be. That's why this community is so special, Reggie. Because we all work to be the best we can be."

"But I don't like the drills."

That stopped her. She felt her confidence slip the slightest bit, and for a moment she could only wait with her hand on the boy's back, wondering why on earth they had put her in charge of these children. She wasn't a mother or even a sibling. Before joining the church, her last job had been waiting at a pizza joint, one of those jobs high school kids work during the summer. With both the reverend and the church, she'd found a sense of place, of community and direction. They trusted her, and she trusted everyone else in turn, but she still failed to wrap her head around the reverend's decision to make her a teacher.

Maybe she'd become a parent one day. Already, Carlos had asked her if she ever thought about children. Though she hadn't considered them before he asked, she liked the idea. Carlos loved her, and she loved him. They'd found each other in Sunrise Gardens, yet another of the miracles that made her believe in the community they were building. Still, she refused to fully consider becoming a parent before she was ready. She'd know the right time.

"I know," she said. "They can be a pain. We'll be back soon, though. Then, I have some really fun things planned."

Reggie looked up from the book. "Like what?"

"It's a surprise. We need to go to assembly in order to find out. Now, do you want to line up with the other kids?"

The boy turned his eyes back to the book. For a moment, he didn't move, and Elizabeth searched her brain for some other track to use, but then he snapped it shut and set it aside. "Okay," he said. He got up and joined the others.

She opened the classroom door, and sunlight streamed in to kiss her face. "Follow close," she said. Then, she led the children outside.

A road carved through the buildings they'd spent the last year constructing. Solid structures that withstood the jungle weather. Recent rains had transformed the dirt thoroughfare to mud, and Elizabeth knew by the time they reached the pavilion, both her and the kids would be filthy. Not that the children would mind. With them, dirtier was always better. She remembered the same policy from her own childhood, Saturday afternoons spent in rainstorms and mud puddles, splashing and laughing, dancing in the muck with nothing in front of her but possibility.

She cast her eyes toward the far west field, where Carlos would be working. Now and then, she worried about him. The worst she could do when exhausted was snap at the kids or doze off in front of them. Carlos worked to clear trees and brush, and she couldn't help but think a chainsaw and lack of sleep were a bad mix. And the recent drills had been so hard on him. She saw him try to be brave, and she appreciated the effort, but she wanted him to know he could unburden himself to her. A front only created stress. They were partners. Together, they could weather anything.

Another series of blasts from the air horn snapped her free of her concern. Instead, a new sour feeling shuddered through her, something guilty and dark, and she slammed a door on it before it could wholly escape. She took her spot at the front of the line and led the children into the road. For a moment, she couldn't bear to look over her shoulder to make sure the children were following.

Just a drill, she told herself. *That's all. Yep.*

THE MUD SUCKED AT her feet. Even overcast, the sky hurt her exhausted eyes. Behind her, the children splashed with each step, not so much walking as stomping. Soon, they'd be muck-covered monstrosities. Still, Elizabeth slapped on a brave face and led her children. Service was about doing her job, so she would do it to the best of her ability.

"Don't splash, kids," she said. A few of them listened, Reggie among them. She felt a tiny swell of pride, swallowed it.

Her smile grew as she saw two elderly men on the side of the road. She knew the best friends as Mr. Redmond and Mr. Tannen, but they always told her to call them Walter and Stan. As she approached, Walter held out his arms as though he were waltzing and took a few clumsy steps, his old hips swiveling.

"I wish they'd change the rhythm. I can't dance to this."

Stan laughed. A hand-rolled cigarette dangled from his lip. Reaching up, he patted his bald head, the sun spots there a little darker today. "You couldn't dance to Count Basie if you had that J. Lo on one arm and Beyonce on the other."

"J. Lo? Which one is that?"

"You know…"

"Elizabeth! Which one is J. Lo? Am I supposed to know who that is?"

She felt her cheeks flare. "Um, she's the one with the butt."

"The really weird rapper?"

"That's Nicky Minaj. Jennifer Lopez is Latina."

Walter froze in mid-swivel. "Wait, so J. Lo and Jennifer Lopez are the same person?"

"Yeah."

"You didn't know that?" Stan asked. His cigarette jumped up and down.

"Don't matter. If I had those two on my arms, I wouldn't be trying to dance."

Stan gave him a wink. "Like you could do the other, either."

"Do it or die trying. What a way to go." He clapped and then held out his hands and looked to the sky. "I'm waiting, Lord. Just remember I'm seventy-four. Don't keep me waiting too long."

Stan bit down on his smoke and flicked it with a finger, sending ash to the ground. "God doesn't work that way."

Walter went back to his clumsy dance. "Don't be so sure. Mysterious ways are called mysterious for a reason."

Elizabeth bit down on the laugh that wanted to explode outward. "We should get going. Signal says urgent."

Walter threw his friend a grin. "Everything's urgent at our age. That's why we get diapers." He started walking, arms back in his dance position.

"Speak for yourself, old man," Stan said. "Won't find none of them things on me."

"Well, don't you just tinkle luck? Give it time. You're still a boy, yet."

"I'm sixty-nine years old."

"And you got the attitude of somebody over a century. Live a little."

Stan nodded past him. "Think it's an option? Living a little, I mean."

Like Walter, Elizabeth followed Stan's eyes and found Tommy, one of Reverend Shaw's closest advisors, wrestling a heavy cart through the mud. His thick arms flexed, body going rigid as he shoved it down the roadway, the stack of boxes and buckets balanced on top swaying with each movement. Marnie, who ran their medical facility, walked beside him, her eyes cast down. Elizabeth felt all her insides tighten at once.

Nervously, she looked for Carlos. When they'd signaled for the previous drill, he'd all but panicked. If she could only look into his eyes, she might feel better. She might be able to convince him everything was okay, maybe even convince herself.

"Go find your parents," she told the kids. They scampered off, oblivious to what Stan had pointed out.

"They bring the cart every time," Walter said. His hand appeared on her back, comforting.

"I know," she said. Her voice sounded smaller than usual.

Stan flicked his cigarette again. Hot ash sizzled in the mud. "Looks fuller than last few times."

"Maybe Tommy wants to show off his arms?"

A shrug. "If I had those arms…"

"Right. Those arms and J. Lo's derriere, right?"

"Ha!" He crammed a whole lot of spite into that syllable. "Think he needs a couple of old gentlemen to help him?"

"I somehow doubt it," Walter said. "Let's go. It's cooling off. I want a spot in the pavilion in case it rains."

"Sure." Stan stubbed out his cigarette and then field stripped it, tucking the remaining paper and filter into his pocket.

Walter gave her back another pat. "It's nothing, sweetie. Another drill, okay? Go find Carlos and hold his hand. You two doing all right?"

"Yes, we're fine. He worries, but I think a lot of us do."

"He's lucky he has you."

"Thank you, Mr. Redmond."

"Walter."

"Walter. Yes, we're doing great."

"That's good. I like seeing young love. It's a great thing, you know."

She smiled despite the nervous feeling in her belly. "I know."

He gave her a grin that looked a little sad, and then he walked toward the pavilion. As she followed, she cast another look at Marnie. She didn't like the woman's expression. Not one bit. Something about it made things feel a little too realistic. The sadness there, the determination, it gave her a sick feeling she didn't like.

A shiver tumbled through her, and she shook it off, decided to look for Carlos instead. She wanted to hold his hand and tell him she loved him. If he could understand, then maybe she could, too.

"REGGIE SAYS HE WAS trouble this morning."

Elizabeth stopped scanning the crowd for Carlos—why hadn't he appeared yet?—and turned to face Reggie's aunt. Though a thin smile decorated her face, it was one of both annoyance and apology.

"He was fine, Mrs. Winters. I think he's just tired. We're all going on too little sleep after last night." For an instant, she looked past the woman, fanning herself as she sweat in the tropical heat. "Everybody's a little on edge, right? We just correct and do our best."

"That's so true."

"Between you and me, I think the drills are really scaring him."

Mrs. Winters' eyes drifted toward the pavilion floor. The sadness in them carried weight.

"He's still doing well with his lessons," Elizabeth said. "Between you and me, he's one of my favorites."

"Thank you, dear. That's very sweet of you." She heaved a heavy breath. "I tried to get my sister to come with Reggie and me. Don't know how many times I told her what a paradise it would be, how amazing the church is and how incredible our community will be. It is, too. I'm not trying to say it isn't. Telling truth, though? I wanted help with Reggie. He can be a handful, I know, and sometimes I get real tired."

Before Elizabeth spared a second thought, she wrapped her arms around Mrs. Winters and hugged her close. "I know, and it's okay. We're all exhausted. That's what good work does, right? Reggie is such a sweet kid. Didn't you say he told on himself?"

Her smile looked a little less sad. "Yeah. Little booger can't get away with nothing."

She leaned in conspiratorially. "Don't tell Reggie, but I'm going to let the kids nap if we're back before the end of classes."

Mrs. Winters turned a key at the corner of her mouth. She cast a look over her shoulder, and when Elizabeth followed she saw Reggie. Hands in his pockets, he kicked at the pavilion's wooden floor. His face was either a mask of fear or boredom.

"I better get us a seat," Mrs. Winters said.

"Sure thing. Hold Reggie close."

The woman nodded and then collected her nephew, led him through the crowd toward one of the many wooden benches that served as pews.

Elizabeth jumped as a hand clamped down on her shoulder. She bit back the scream that almost broke free, swallowed it as she turned to see Carlos's wide eyes boring into hers.

"You're safe," he said. "Thank God."

She placed a hand on his cheek. Sweat soaked his skin, and his hands trembled a little against her arms. Fear filled his eyes. "Of course, I am," she said. "It's just a drill, Carlos. Just another drill."

"That's not what I heard." His eyes darted back and forth. "I heard it's bad this time."

"It's bad every time." She struggled to keep her voice calm. Why was he so scared? He'd been unnerved in the past, anxious, but this was something new. Carlos looked close to panic. His eyes–slate gray and normally so sad–grew wilder by the second, and he kept flipping his black hair out of his eyes in a way she'd never seen before. Everything about him looked manic. "Besides, you were out in the field. How could you hear anything when they just called the assembly ten minutes ago?"

When his hands clamped down hard on her arms, she almost screamed again. His eyes still searching the crowd, he ushered her toward the pavilion's edge. The crowd was thinner there, the last stragglers just now reaching the meeting.

He leaned in close, his voice hushed. "We saw two trucks leave. It was maybe twenty, thirty minutes ago. Their beds were full of men, at least six each. They had guns, Elizabeth. Like, big ones."

She tried to swallow, only to realize her mouth had gone dry. "That doesn't–"

"What if Father Shaw thinks people will try to leave?"

The sudden desire to shake her head, to tell him the reverend wouldn't do that, filled her, but she'd been at the other drills. She'd seen the way Reverend Shaw could get when people didn't see the light. Just a week before, she'd watched as Tommy held a shining pistol to the temple of Ellie Martins when she refused to drink. She remembered the tense, almost electric feeling in her stomach as she watched and waited, how relief had crashed through her when Ellie finally held the paper cup to her lips and sipped.

Faith is a sword, Reverend Shaw had said. *Sometimes it needs to be forged in fire.*

"We'll see, all right?" she said. "Try to remember your faith."

"I will. I just…I'm scared, Elizabeth."

"Me too. We'd be idiots if we weren't."

"Are we idiots if we stay?"

She thought about the answer too long, a few quick seconds that proved she felt doubt. Around her, the community continued to trickle in, the last few finally arriving from the farthest fields, but she suddenly felt miles away, isolated. Her first moment of doubt, and she hated it. She felt weak and worthless. A betrayer.

"No," she said. "We're a part of this community, and we built something great here. We won't abandon it." She slipped her hands inside his. "It'll be fine, no matter what. All we need is right here."

Before she could say anything else, canned organ music blasted through the sound system loud enough to crackle at the edges. A cheer rose through the pavilion. Its power struck Elizabeth in the chest. She heard awe and excitement and love in that roar, but, for the first time, she heard something else, too. Was there also a note of desperation? Of fear? Shaking her head, she told herself she was just tired, fatigue making her imagine things that weren't there.

LEADING CARLOS BY THE hand, she found seats near the back of the pavilion. Those around them clapped. As she watched, a relieved smile broke across Carlos's face, and then he jammed two fingers into his mouth and whistled. Good. His faith remained strong. She joined in the applause.

WHAT HAPPENED AT SUNRISE GARDENS

She craned her neck to peer past those in front of her, and she smiled at Reverend Shaw's approach. He crossed the lawn between his cabin and the pavilion, his assistant Rita walking alongside him, her hand on his arm. A smile filled his face, and he lifted a hand to wave well before he reached the pulpit, eliciting more cheers from the congregation. His smile comforted her. It was another drill, nothing more. She gave Carlos's arm a good squeeze, and he grinned. A second later, however, his expression crumpled, worry crashing in once more.

"What?" she asked.

"Rita. Look."

She checked the woman's face, and what she saw there made her body wash cold. Rita's expression, usually friendly if a little cool, was a mask of despair. Red ringed her eyes, and her lips trembled as she walked alongside the reverend. Something was wrong, so wrong it had shaken one of Shaw's most trusted devotees.

"It's really not a drill," she said.

"No, it isn't."

Her hand fell from Carlos's arm. She felt weightless, and her vision blurred. For several seconds, she thought she'd either float away or collapse to the ground. Only when she bit down on her tongue did her eyes clear and her equilibrium return.

Mentally, she ran through the rules as Reverend Shaw had written them. First, there would be an explanation. He would tell the congregation why they all needed to do it (she couldn't quite make herself think *why they all needed to die*). Then, there would be a discussion and open forum. Pros and cons would be weighed, and doubters could air their doubts without fear of reproach. Finally, they would all line up and drink. There would be a minute of pain, and then there would be nothing.

Interesting, she thought for the first time. *Step two doesn't seem to have any effect on step three.* She felt a quick swell of self-loathing for her doubt, but shook it off.

I just hope it doesn't hurt the children. Please don't let it hurt the children.

The dark thoughts taunted her, but she refused to let them take deeper root. The reverend and his church had saved her, and she owed her life and her salvation to both. If anything, she owed the church her confidence and faith. She knew the real truth, though. She owed the church—she owed Reverend Shaw—her life.

THE FLORIDA SUN—A RED angry sliver cresting the horizon—burned her sensitive eyes. Her head throbbed with the previous night's vodka, cheap well drinks from a bar on the south side of town. As she climbed free of her car, she struggled to remember its name, but her thoughts ping ponged too fast for her to remember. She had the panic to thank for that.

Her stomach clenched. She fought to breathe through it, but could only gasp. A quartet of panicked breaths, and then she collapsed to all fours and vomited across the pavement. The smell of strong alcohol twisted her guts again, and she coughed up a second round.

"Fuck," she said. With the back of her hand, she wiped a stream of bile from her chin. She climbed to her feet, and the feel of concrete against her soles told her she'd left her shoes in the car. For a moment, she considered going back for them. Best she could figure, she still had a couple of miles to walk before she made it home. A look at her Camry, however, its grill wrapped around the lightpost and coolant pouring onto the sidewalk told her she didn't have time. At the moment, her only options were start walking or hang out and do a lot of explaining. Not much of a decision at all.

She scurried away, putting as much distance as she could between the wreck and herself. When she reached the first intersection, she ducked to the right. At the next intersection she took a left. A part of her knew the car could be traced to her, but she didn't care. She cared about nothing but distance, escape.

The sidewalk bit at her feet. She ignored the pain, just kept walking, telling herself not to run the same way she fought to keep from chewing on her lip in a nervous frenzy. On more than one occasion, she'd failed, found herself with lips that bled for days, trying to cover them with lipstick as she smiled for customers at the pizza place. Over the past year, she'd grown used to it, same as she'd grown used to acting like she wasn't half-drunk while she served pizza and breadsticks and cold beer.

"Good job coping," she said. With three blocks between herself and her wrecked car, she leaned against a lightpost, breathed deep. Her mouth twisted into a sneer and then a frown, and her eyes stung with tears. Dammit, she'd crashed her car. She'd tried to drive home with a system full of vodka, and she'd slammed the thing right into a pole. Somebody was going to find it, and the cops were going to trace it right back to her. How was she going to get out of this mess? Maybe she could say it was stolen, or that she was concussed and stumbled away. Neither explanation held a lot of water, but they were all her burning mind could conjure.

"Goddammit!" The first sob shook her entire body, and before she could stop herself she turned and slammed her forehead into the metal post. Stars erupted, and the pain drove her to one knee. At least maybe her concussion story would work now. Instead of feeling a sense of relief, she rubbed her forehead and cursed herself for being an idiot.

Stumbling, trying to navigate with blurred and fizzling vision, she continued down the street. A bed waited at the end of her journey, and with any luck she could get some sleep before the police arrived. At the very least, it was more time for the alcohol to leave her system.

She touched a hand to her forehead, and it came away stained with blood. Not a lot, but enough to know her pole maneuver had done some damage. More than once, she looked over her shoulder, considered turning around and walking back to the wreck. The cops had to be there by now. With the blood on her face, her story might be believable. Sure, the cops would test her, realize she had alcohol in her system, but a weekend in the drunk tank had to be better than the other consequences she'd racked up.

The blipping of a police siren cut the air as she was still trying to decide. Panic stabbing her, she turned to see the patrol car pull up to the curb in front of her. For a single instant, she considered running, but the idea shattered as soon as it came together. Fleeing would just make things worse.

"Dammit. Goddammit." Gasping, she tried to swallow the sobs that bubbled up her throat, but she couldn't. They came one after the other, and when the tears stole her vision, she saw nothing but a ruined future.

"Ma'am?"

She heard the voice, heard the car door open immediately after, but everything was a blur. Her lips curled back, and another sob bent her in half. This was it. Nowhere left to go but down.

"Ma'am, are you okay?"

"No."

Slowly, she sat on the sidewalk and lowered her bleeding face into her hands.

THE CHEERS SWELLED AS Reverend Shaw stepped to the pulpit two parishioners had spent a month crafting by hand, all darkly stained wood and smooth edges, a lighter cross hanging from the front. He wore a black shirt, the same loose style he'd always worn since they'd relocated to Central America. Sunglasses obscured the eyes just above his smile, but he soon took them off, setting them on the pulpit and retrieving a pair of reading glasses from a pocket. A frown replaced his smile as he leaned forward.

"I wanted to get a good look at everyone," he said. His voice quivered.

Laughter rippled through the pavilion as the congregation sat. Elizabeth thought some of it sounded nervous.

"I love you all. You know that right?"

The replies rang out from every corner.

"We know, Father!"

"Amen!"

"And we love you!"

"Hallelujah!"

"Your love sustains us!"

"Please," Reverend Shaw said. "It's God's love that sustains you. I only deliver His word."

She swallowed hard and held Carlos's hand tighter. His free hand patted her arm. Perhaps he meant it to be a comforting gesture, but instead it filled her with an awful knowledge and urgency. Each touch could be her last. The questions followed. Would it really only hurt for a minute? Would Carlos be able to hold her as their bodies shook? What would they do to those who refused to drink? A breath shuddered out of her as she remembered the shining gun. She knew exactly what would happen.

A look at Rita and Tommy made her wonder. They stood beside each other, hands clasped and heads slightly bowed, Shaw's closest assistants. Would they force the poison down their throats? Time would tell.

Why was she even thinking these thoughts? Her faith remained strong. She refused to fear death, for it was only the beginning of paradise.

The reverend took a step back from the pulpit. Looking over the congregation, his smile returned, but it looked more than a little forced. He held up both hands, asking for quiet, and the remaining voices fell silent.

He propped his elbows on the lectern and interlaced his fingers, leaned in as if about to pray. Instead, he spoke. "When I look at what we've done here—the amazing accomplishment of bringing together all these wonderful people and the building of this community, the staking out of our own place where we can be free and experience even a little bit of paradise here on earth—I find myself filled with great pride. Now, I know pride is a sin. You know that, too. What can I say? No man is perfect. I am just as human as every one of you. Just as prone to sin and desire and fallibility. It is how we accept each other and our terrible, human flaws that marks us for forgiveness in the world ever after."

Applause filled the air. Despite her fears, Elizabeth found herself clapping along. The smile on her face felt natural and good.

Reverend Shaw drew a handkerchief from his pocket and wiped his brow. He sniffled and then wiped at his nose. "What we've created here, it lets us truly be free. There is no tax, here. No man or woman or child gives any more than what they want, and all of you have given so freely. Your work—your support of the community—is what has allowed us in Sunrise Gardens to thrive. This makes my heart glad. Here, we are not subject to the antiquated and unfair laws of what sinners like to call the civilized world. There are no minorities here; every last one of us is their brother's equal. No laws exist to keep the lower classes in their place or to oppress women. We do not live to prop up a cruel an unfair status quo.

"For so long, I have feared an attack from outside our borders. We all have, I know. Though we have declared our sovereignty from that land of decadence and corruption, the United States government still feels it holds sway over us. I know we have prepared for such an eventuality, have feared that one day that twisted engine might come and try to mow us down, and I know we all accept what must be done to guarantee our journey to paradise when that happens. And I am sorry—I swear to you all, with God as my witness, that I am so sorry—but such a day has come."

A rumble of worried voices rolled through the pavilion. Somebody screamed. Elizabeth saw a teenage boy slump forward and then crash to the floor, and then she shut her eyes. Carlos pulled her to him, and she kissed his cheek.

"Don't be scared," he whispered.

"I'm not."

"Discussion!" someone shouted.

Reverend Shaw held up his hands. "There will be discussion; we've always promised ourselves this. We have rules, and we will abide by those rules. Don't worry."

The reverend rubbed his sinuses. His face looked pained. "Honestly, I'm not sure how to tell all of you this. For so long, we expected the end of our community to come from outside government aggression. It's no secret that the fascists of this world hate us for the free society we've created. They have no power here, and fascists love nothing more than holding power in their cold, steel fists. The fact that they hold no sway here must fill them with more rage than they know how to handle.

"But...I'm serious—I don't know how to tell you this. What our community faces right now is a much graver threat than any government. Perhaps a government we could fight or negotiate with in some way. What we're facing now...maybe it's best if I don't try to tell you. I've been monitoring the news across the world, and yesterday a series of disturbing reports started surfacing. I recorded some of them, and I'd like to play them for you now. I'll warn you now that they're quite disturbing. However, I do feel it's for the best that you all listen. They will explain the gravity of the situation far better than I can with mere words."

A frown stitched Elizabeth's face. Her grip on Carlos's hand tightened another notch.

Reverend Shaw signaled to one of his assistants, who then leaned over the public address system and started playing a tape.

Static hissed and popped through the speakers for several seconds, and then a newscaster's voice filled the pavilion.

"The National Guard has been deployed in New York, Los Angeles, Chicago, St. Louis, and Dallas in an attempt to quell the violence in our nation's most dangerous hot spots. The President has said he remains confident that order can be restored."

A different voice cut in. *"Attacks now being reported in London and Paris and Mexico City. Pockets of violence are also being reported in Rio de Janeiro. This unprecedented epidemic appears to be spreading with no end in sight."*

Another voice. *"Reports coming in now that those killed by these cannibalistic attackers are reanimating. This...it doesn't seem possible, but reports are widespread and coming in by the second. As awful as it seems, it appears the dead are rising to attack the living."*

The reverend signaled to his assistants, who stopped the recording. A troubled murmur filled the pavilion, and everywhere Elizabeth looked she saw faces of fear and disbelief. Beside her, Carlos shook his head, saying something under his breath. From what she could hear, Elizabeth thought it was a prayer.

"I know it's troubling," Reverend Shaw said. "I'm troubled by it as well. When I heard the first reports three days ago, I could hardly believe them myself. We live in the real world, not a universe of horror films and science fiction fantasies. The dead do not rise to kill the living; I know this, and you know this. Though I was troubled, I waited until I knew for sure before bringing this information to the rest of you. You see, I had to know. I had to ask God, and I had to be sure.

"Sadly, I am sure. When the dead rise, it is the first sign of The End, the great apocalypse where Hell itself will wash over the earth and consume us all with its fires. There will be other signs. The skies will shatter. The waters will boil. Demons will join the dead to tear apart those of us still alive, and no holiness will save us. This mortal world is over, I'm afraid. There is nothing we can do to stop this."

Someone had started sobbing. Elizabeth couldn't find them, but the hitching sound of their cries rolled across the pavilion like the beginning of an avalanche. Others joined. Someone shouted, but she couldn't make out the word. Something had started buzzing in her ears, an almost mechanical humming that she thought might be her mind overloading. When the reverend spoke again, his voice sounded raw and electric, spitting and sparking at the edges.

"I know we all suspected the day to take action would come, and I know we all thought it would come for another reason. Once, we thought the taking of our own lives would be revolutionary, a final stand against the tyranny of evil men. Instead, we find ourselves at a strange crossroads, a place where our deaths will spare us both the horrors to come and an eternity spent walking this world as demons who feast on flesh.

"For make no mistake, good people. I've never lied to you, and I'm not lying to you now. Though we may be isolated, and though we may be protected, the dead will come. They will make their way here, and they will wash over us like the great flood. I refuse to watch those I care about—who care for each other—become nothing more than meat for a tide of beasts. After all we've done and how far we've journeyed, we deserve better. We deserve to leave this dying planet and ascend to God's kingdom on our own terms, at a time and place of our choosing. God granted us with free will not to test us, but so that we may join

Him when the time comes. The hour of flesh has ended, and the hour of The Spirit is upon us, my friends. When the time comes to drink, then all must drink. It is the only way to save ourselves from terror and torment."

The murmur exploded all at once, angry and confused voices battering each other like prizefighters. Elizabeth tried to decide how she felt, what she'd do or say, but her thoughts bounced from one place to the next before she could snatch them. What Reverend Shaw had told them...what sense did it make? The dead rising? Eating the living? She'd seen enough movies that she knew the trope, and the switch in her head that might let her believe it refused to flip. But Reverend Shaw had never lied to her, had never lied to any of them. The frown stitched onto her face hurt almost as much as the ache in her mind and heart.

Again, Reverend Shaw held up his hands. Slowly, the congregation quieted, returning to the troubled rumble from a moment before.

"I know this is a lot to take in," he said, "and I wish I had any other way of telling you. In light of these...disturbing circumstances...discussion will begin an hour from now. I encourage you to spend the next sixty minutes with your friends and loved ones. Think about what you've heard and gather your thoughts. Pray. I expect our discussion will be both difficult and comprehensive, but I know we will reach the correct decision, and then we will remove ourselves from Armageddon's path and ascend to meet God in Heaven."

Waving, Reverend Shaw stepped away from the pulpit. His head bowed, he let Rita slip an arm inside his, and together they left the pavilion, ignoring the dozens of voices calling out to him.

Carlos called once, but Elizabeth couldn't understand his voice over the din. All she heard was the note of his voice, confusion that bordered on terror.

She shook her head, clearing some of the jumbled thoughts. Around her, the community's voices mashed into chaos. If they would just be quiet for a moment, she could make sense of everything. Just a minute to think. She didn't need any more.

"We should go to the cabin," she told Carlos. "We have an hour, so we can talk a bit, get ready."

"Won't the kids need you?"

"The kids will need their parents. And their parents will need them. I need you."

His smile reassured her some. When they'd first reached the pavilion, she'd thought he might be crumbling. Considering what was happening to the world—as difficult as it was to believe—she liked seeing his resolve return. It bolstered her strength. Without a second thought, she wrapped her arms around him and pulled him close.

"I love you," she said.

"And I love you."

She began to smile, but then a piercing scream slashed the expression from her face. As she whipped away from Carlos, the first panicked thought to shoot through her brain was *They're already here!* Sunrise Gardens sat in the middle of the jungle. How could they be attacked so quickly?

When Reggie ran from the pavilion, screaming, "No! No! No!" she realized the truth of the matter, and she took after him even as her heart cracked a little wider. As she splashed into the muddy street, she thought she heard Carlos behind her, but she refused to take her eyes off the boy. He bounced off a woman, nearly sending her toppling, and simply spun and kept running, kept shrieking terrified notes into the air.

"Reggie, come back!" she said. If he heard her over his fear, he chose to ignore her. The mud grabbed at her ankles, and she struggled to stay upright, but she refused to abandon the chase. She needed to comfort Reggie, needed to get him safely back to his aunt.

So they can die together.

Shut up!

They were halfway back to the classroom when the mud finally dragged down Reggie. He landed with a violent splash. Instead of scrambling back to his feet, wrestling his way free of the muck, he curled into a tight ball and wailed.

Elizabeth reached him a second later, all but throwing herself on top of the boy. She took him in her arms and tried to wipe the mud from his face. "It's okay," she said. "It's going to be okay."

The mud was cold, but Elizabeth didn't care. She held Reggie in her arms and told him over and over again that everything would be fine. Slowly, he stopped fighting and went limp in her embrace. Carlos knelt beside them, patting Reggie's head and looking at her in concern.

"It's okay," she said again. This time, she held Carlos with her eyes. He nodded.

Reggie shivered, so she pulled him closer. Maybe they should get out of the muddy street, but she didn't think the boy was ready yet. Trying to do too much might set off another panic attack. Her heart ached for the boy. He was too young, his brain still crowded with memories from the life before Sunrise Gardens. How could he understand? How could he be anything other than terrified?

She kept whispering to Reggie. Mrs. Winters looked both concerned and embarrassed as she slogged through the muck to reach them. "I'm so sorry," she said. "Baby, are you all right?"

"He's scared," Elizabeth said. "Understandable. It's really fine."

Mrs. Winters crouched beside her nephew. With her hands, she rubbed his upper arms, and his shivering calmed some. "There's nothing to be scared of. It's going to be okay."

"But there are monsters," he said. His grit teeth distorted the words.

"They're far away. We're all alone out here. They're never going to get here."

"Then why do we have to...?" A sob strangled the sentence, and he started trembling again.

Elizabeth's stomach clenched, and everything felt weightless. Her arms went limp around the boy, and as his aunt took him, she wondered how such a thing could possibly be explained.

"We're taking matters into our own hands," Mrs. Winters said. "We came here to be free, right? This is how we're going to be free."

Finally, Reggie opened his eyes. They grew wide and pleading as he looked at his aunt and then to Elizabeth and back again.

"Do you understand?" she asked.

"But..."

"What is it, baby?"

"I don't want to die."

Elizabeth slumped into the mud, and even Carlos's arms wrapping around her failed to keep the chill at bay.

WHAT HAPPENED AT SUNRISE GARDENS

"IT'S GOING TO BE okay," Carlos said. His voice remained even and caring, but his hand on her shoulder felt more irritating than anything. She knew he was trying to help, but, as she did her best to clean the mud from her hair, all she could think of was Reggie's terrified voice.

I don't want to die.

How could she explain it to the boy? She remembered her own childhood, how everything seemed so endless and wonderful and full of potential. If someone had told her then that it would all end in a few short hours, she would have reacted in much the same way. But how would she react to learning monsters weren't only real, but were on their way?

"I'm not sure the reverend handled it right," she said. "Discussion will be difficult enough without the children being terrified. Letting them know complicates things."

Carlos nodded, his expression thoughtful and solemn. "True. He wanted to respect them, though. Everyone's equal here, right? That includes the children. They have the right to know."

"Of course, they do. There's a big difference between having the right to hear something and the ability to understand it, though."

"I get that. Hopefully, he'll understand."

"I hope so." She wiped a few tears from her eyes. When Carlos sat beside her, she rested her head on his shoulder. "How do you think discussion will go?"

"I guess we'll see."

She took hold of his hand and squeezed. "I thought we'd get married."

"Me too."

"I wish there was still time."

"We could ask Reverend Shaw?"

"Are you serious?" She smiled. When she looked to Carlos, he smiled, too. It was a good idea. Maybe it would help the entire congregation, lighten the mood the slightest bit?

Carlos climbed off the bed and dropped to his knee in front of her. His hands felt hot, and when she looked in his eyes, she saw him through a scrim of happy tears. Her breath caught in her throat as he spoke.

"I don't have a ring. Sorry for that. Elizabeth Daniels, I love you very much. If I could spend the rest of my time as your husband, it would be the greatest gift I've ever received. Will you marry me?"

Her smile grew, and she managed to ignore the swell of grief in her chest. "Yes," she said.

For a second, his gaze dropped to the floor. He sniffled before lifting his head again. "Do you think…? It's…maybe it's not as bad as it sounded, you know? What if we–"

She placed her hands on his cheek. Her smile wavered a little, but held. "Baby, we chose this. We're here with our community, our family. You know the same as me we can't just leave."

"I know."

Leaning forward, she kissed his forehead. "We'll get married, and it will be amazing. Maybe the honeymoon won't be as long as we would've liked, but we'll be man and wife in the end. Won't that be amazing?"

"Yeah. It will be."

She moved to kiss his lips, but a knock on their cabin door froze her in place. "Timing, right?" she said, wrenching a tiny chuckle from Carlos.

Mrs. Winters waited on her cabin's stoop. Reggie stood at her side, eyes cast toward the ground. Mud remained caked on his face and hair.

"Hi," she said.

"I was hoping I could talk," Mrs. Winters said.

She motioned the pair into the cabin. "Come on in." She gave Reggie a smile as he entered behind his aunt. He stood close to the woman, half-hidden behind her hip. With both his hands, he held hers. "How are you doing, Reggie?"

"He's still scared. I think he's a little embarrassed, too."

Just as she had in the classroom, she knelt beside the boy. "There's nothing to be embarrassed about. What you did, a lot of people probably wanted to do that. They might be a little jealous, if anything." She reached out to wipe some of the crusted mud from his face, but he flinched away.

"Sorry," Mrs. Winters said. "He's not talking much. Everything's still...raw."

"I get it. It's okay, Reggie. Don't tell anybody else, but you're one of my favorite students. You're a great kid." She hoped her words might get something out of him—a smile, or at least to stop clutching at his aunt—but instead he kept his eyes toward the floor. He shivered a little. The movement brought a frown to her face. She searched for the right words, anything that might make the reality of their situation easier for him. Instead, Mrs. Winters' voice pulled her eyes upward.

"We're leaving. He wanted to say goodbye."

"What? You can't—"

She held up a hand. Her face was calm, almost stone. "I know what you're going to say, and I'm going to ask you not to. I've thought about this long and hard, and you're not going to change my mind. Yes, I understand why you might. I won't criticize you for your belief. This is mine, though. The only member of my family I have left. His mother…she begged me to keep him safe."

Carlos stepped forward. "There are guns. I saw men go out in trucks."

"I don't care." Her mouth formed a tight line. Her eyes squeezed shut. With her free hand, she reached over and patted Reggie. In response, he nuzzled closer to her hip. "We know it's a chance, but we're going to take it."

"You heard the reports," Elizabeth said. "If you're going to make a choice…"

Mrs. Winters took an abrupt step forward, bringing herself within a foot of Elizabeth. "I am making a choice. I am choosing to not make my nephew drink."

For a moment, she held the woman's gaze, and she thought maybe the pure force of her resolve could crack the woman, shatter her doubt and restore her faith. The steel in her eyes made Elizabeth look away, however, and when she did, she found Reggie wide and wet and shivering.

"You heard Carlos," she said. "The guns." She wanted to believe the men Carlos had seen were out to protect the community. The doubt in her heart filled her with guilt.

"I heard."

"Okay. We…we won't say anything. I promise."

"Thank you. There's something else, though." With both hands, she hugged her nephew's head. "I won't lie, it's a lot."

Elizabeth waited, watching as Mrs. Winters looked around the cabin, suddenly afraid to meet her eyes. Her nerves crackled. Whatever it was, it had to be something big.

"I'm old," she said. "I ain't gonna lie about that. My joints burn on my best days. I get tired a lot easier than I care to say. As much as I hate to admit it, we won't get far at all if he has to depend on me. Someone else needs to come."

"Wait," Carlos said. "You can't be saying—"

"I'm not. I'm asking. There are people here I trust, but most of them are my age, maybe a little younger. I trust you though, Elizabeth. Reggie trusts you. Like you said earlier, he's a good boy. If he trusts you, then I trust you.

"I'm sorry. What I'm asking, it sounds crazy. I know that. What the reverend played for us sounds crazy too, though. If it's not real, then that doesn't make it any less crazy. Think about that for a minute.

"Really, I just want Reggie to have a chance. He's just a boy. You can't tell me he doesn't deserve a chance. I wish I could give him that chance. More than anything, I wish I could, but I can't. If he has to depend on me, he won't have a chance at all. You can give him that chance, though. I'm so sorry I have to ask, but you're the only chance he has. Please, Elizabeth. Help Reggie have a chance."

Stunned, Elizabeth took a step back. She felt Carlos touch her back, but she didn't turn to face him. Instead, her eyes ticked back and forth between Reggie and his aunt. Her thoughts felt slippery. They writhed through her brain and refused to calm. She suddenly felt cold, and a shiver just like Reggie's ran through her.

"I...Mrs. Winters..."

"It's a lot. I know that. Believe me, if there was some other way, I'd do it, but there just isn't. There isn't much time. I'm begging you, Elizabeth. Please do this."

She swallowed, and the sound was a rumble in her ears. When she looked at Reggie again, a plea filled his eyes. That plea struck her right in the chest, almost stealing her breath. How was she supposed to answer him? What could she possibly say? How do you explain to a child that choosing to die was the noble decision?

Again, she reached out to touch Reggie. This time, he didn't flinch. When her fingers grazed his shoulder, she felt his skin tremble. Either cold or fear had his nerves twitching, and she didn't think it particularly mattered which was the culprit. The result was all the same. Slowly, she placed her entire hand against his skin, trying to comfort him.

"Reggie, I..." The rest of the words caught in her throat. All that came out was a single, "Damn."

"We were going to ask the reverend to marry us," Carlos said. He let the words hang like an explanation.

"He won't do it," Mrs. Winters said. Something like pity floated in her eyes. "I been down here longer than you, came down to escape a whole lot of hate. Trust me, I really thought this place was gonna be the answer. My sister thought the exact same thing. I been here long enough, though, I realize what it really is. This whole place—Sunrise Gardens—it's just a pillar to that man's ego. He won't marry you because it ain't about him."

Elizabeth shook her head. She felt almost insulted. "You can't mean that. The reverend, he brought us all here. He offered us an alternative to all the bad things back there. You can't really—"

"How many times have we practiced? Answer me that. How many times has he lined us all up, kept us on our feet for hours in the middle of the night when we're sore and exhausted, and then asked us to drink? Do you really think he does that because he thinks it's best for us? You're young, and you're idealistic, but you're not stupid, Elizabeth. When he does that, he's making sure we'd do anything for him.

"Have you ever seen him work in the fields with Carlos? Has he helped you teach the kids? Do you think he's writing sermons the whole time? That man is nothing but a petty king, and we're nothing but his subjects."

Elizabeth breathed deep. She felt anger throb in her brain like an ember in a sporadic breeze. "I don't know why you're saying these things. If you feel this way, why haven't you left sooner? Why did you go through the other drills?"

"Why now?" Carlos asked.

"Why now? You can't really be asking that question. Why are you two suddenly wanting Shaw to marry you? Just like me, you know this isn't a drill. This is the real deal, and you know when you drink this time, it'll be for the last time. And you're standing there, and you're telling me I should walk my nephew up to a metal tub and tell him to go ahead and take a big gulp because maybe that will make him die a little faster. You're telling me that suicide is what's best for a ten-year-old boy. That's what you're trying to tell me."

Her words threw water on the ember, left it smoking guilt. Elizabeth turned away. She couldn't bear to keep her eyes on Mrs. Winters or Reggie. "I'm not saying that. I don't want...I don't want any of this to happen, but I don't know what to do. Okay? I have no idea what to do!"

A hand touched her cheek, and she found it was her turn to flinch. When she looked, she saw Mrs. Winters reaching for her. "Elizabeth, honey, you're a good girl. And Carlos is a good man.

The truth is, the fact that you don't know what to do is exactly why Reverend Shaw brought you here. He doesn't want people thinking for themselves. That's why we all have our jobs, why everything's for the good of The Gardens. It's...it's one for all, but when we go all for one, that one is always gonna be Shaw.

"Now, I don't know if there are monsters out there eating people. I have my doubts. Really, I just think Shaw found himself a little deeper in something than he can climb out of. I don't know what it could be, and I don't care, but I am not going to let him murder my nephew because of it!"

Elizabeth went to her cot and sat down. Elbows on her knees, she rested her face in her hands. She knew she needed to make a decision. As much as she hated to admit it, the things Mrs. Winters had told her made some sense. When had she last seen the reverend outside a drill or sermon? Over the past several months, he'd shifted away from being a part of the community to being the leader of it. And now he wanted everyone to drink because the dead were returning to eat the living? It sounded insane, and she hated the cracks it formed in her faith.

"Mrs. Winters, I—"

The short-short-long bleating of the urgent signal cut off her words. She turned to Carlos, saw him looking in several directions at once, his head swiveling in confusion. "Has it been an hour?" he asked.

Mrs. Winters looked at her wrist. "Just over twenty minutes. Look at how he's playing it—he promises time to think and decide, and then he doesn't give it. Discussion will go the same way. It might look like a debate, but it won't be. Everyone will have to drink no matter what."

Elizabeth looked out the window, saw the community filter into the street as they started the trek toward the pavilion. "I don't know if this means it's too late to run or the perfect time."

Carlos wrapped his arms around her. "Is that what you want to do?"

"I don't know. What about you?"

"I want to be with you. I go where you go."

Elizabeth leaned against the door. Her hands curling into fists, she rubbed at her eyes and hated that the decision was suddenly hers. To hand her so much responsibility wasn't fair, but she also knew responsibility never cared about such things. It demanded decision and action, and it refused to wait until a better time.

Stars flaring behind her eyelids, she thought back to her life in the United States, how she'd been a drunk and how everything had spiraled right toward the bottom until the day she stumbled into Reverend Shaw's church. She hated to think the first thing she'd believed in could be a lie, but she couldn't deny the doubt that had seeped into her heart. It sat there like a black mass, and with each second it grew. She fought against it, but its spread wouldn't stop, wouldn't slow.

Frowning, she opened her eyes. She had to make a decision, she knew. Breathing deep, she looked from Carlos to Mrs. Winters and finally to Reggie. What could she do? What was the right call?

"Hide here," she said. "Get under the cots and stay put, okay? If…if everything goes bad, you can get out after."

Mrs. Winters' face crumbled. "Elizabeth—"

"I'm sorry. It's the best I can do right now." Everything felt heavy, and her eyes welled with tears.

"What if somebody finds us?" The quiet, frightened sound of Reggie's voice in the cabin struck her like an open hand. He looked at her with those wide eyes and then peered up at his aunt. His fingers tightened around her hand.

She looked to Carlos. His face didn't reveal any answers.

"Don't get caught," she said. "I don't know what else to say."

"We need to go," Carlos said.

"I know." Before she could think twice, she threw her arms around Mrs. Winters and hugged her close. "I'm so sorry," she said. "Maybe I'll see you later."

"I hope so."

She ran a hand over Reggie's muddy hair. "You be brave. I know you can be."

He barely moved, but she thought he might have nodded. Instead of wondering if she'd imagined it, she met Carlos at the door and watched as Mrs. Winters wedged Reggie under the bed and then crawled in after him. The woman gave her a short, hard look that made her feel awful. She almost apologized again, but instead she took Carlos by the hand and left the cabin.

HER ENTIRE HEAD ACHED. Sitting on a bed in the emergency room, staring at the farthest wall without focusing on anything, she thought her throbbing brain might crack her skull, if she hadn't already done the job against the light post. The doctor had said her X-rays didn't show any problems, but the pounding at her temples and forehead and everywhere else told her otherwise. She frowned, the same expression she'd been making for the past hour, and whispered to herself what a goddamn idiot she was.

"You feeling any better?"

When she looked up, she recognized the patrolman who'd either been kind enough to check on a woman bleeding all over the sidewalk or had known she was the asshole who'd abandoned a trashed car after puking vodka all over the pavement. Like a good cop, he carried a steaming cup of coffee in each hand. He handed her one before he pulled up a chair and sat.

"I guessed you like it black," he said.

"Um…okay."

"Fine. You look really hungover. Figured you could use it." One corner of his mouth ticked upward in a facsimile of a smile. Lizzie couldn't tell if he was Cuban or Puerto Rican, but she figured one of the two was correct. He looked handsome, kind, but that could just be some kind of cop maneuver, send in the looker to be nice and gain her trust before someone else drops the hammer. Not that she hadn't earned the drop.

"Thanks," she said. She leaned forward to get a good look at his badge. "Officer Ruiz."

"Call me Tommy."

"Fine. Still, thank you."

Nodding, he watched her over the rim of his paper cup. She waited, trying hard not to look too ashamed. "How's your head?" he asked.

"It hurts."

"I bet. Sounds like you'll be okay, though. No concussion. You're lucky."

"Am I?"

A little shrug. "Could have been worse."

She found it was her turn to shrug. Could it really be worse?

Officer Ruiz took another sip and then made a production of placing his cup on the floor. He leaned back in his chair, crossed his hands across his stomach. "Do I need to dance around the thing with the car?"

"I guess not. Shouldn't a detective or somebody ask about that, though?"

"Technically? Maybe. Everything's backed up, though. Kissimmee has its issues, right? Lot of stuff going down, and it's not like you hurt anybody. Your car's totaled, probably, but you didn't even damage that light post. Lucky break, there."

She chuckled before she could stop herself. "Sorry. I just don't feel lucky."

"You're alive. That's something. You need your silver lining, that's a start. There's a better lining, though."

"Oh, yeah?"

A sigh escaped him as he retrieved his coffee. Another little shrug, smaller than the last. "I'm not gonna lie to you. You were impaired. It's obvious. For all I know, a simple screening could show more than alcohol in your system. Put those together, you could be looking at a pretty serious situation."

Watching him, she tried to think of an explanation, an excuse. A lie. Instead, she said, "Is that the dark part of the cloud?"

"Yeah, and it's pretty dark. Sorry."

She sipped instead of answering. Bitter coffee singed her tongue, and she thought it was the least she deserved.

"What do you think happens now?" Officer Ruiz asked.

"I don't know. Nothing good, probably."

"Not necessarily. I mean, there isn't anything official yet. If we can keep it off the books, it makes things easier for everybody."

There it was. A sudden disgust filled her belly as anger flared behind her eyes. Asshole cop. "Is this the part where I blow you and you let me walk out of here with a warning, or do you need to bend me over the bed?"

"Whoa." He held up both hands, waved her off. "I'm not talking about that at all. I can see...that's not what I'm saying, okay? Not gonna happen."

Lizzie watched him with narrowed eyes. Maybe he was telling the truth, but maybe he was backpedalling. Did he really have to take a step back, though? If he wanted her to work off her crime, she'd either do it or go to jail. Really, just another consequence of what she'd decided to do with her life.

"So, what are you talking about?" she asked.

"I'm talking about you getting sober, straightening out your life a little. Sound good?"

"I guess. I've certainly heard worse."

"Okay, then." He leaned forward, fished a leather wallet from his back pocket. A few flicks of his fingers, and he withdrew a business card, handed it over to her between two fingers. "Well, this could be a good first step."

Tentatively, she plucked the card from his fingers. Holding it horizontally, she saw the bottom third was black, the top two thirds blue, a sky hugging an artificial horizon. Written in gold across the field of blue were the words *SUNRISE MINISTRIES*. A local address stretched across the bottom, also in gold.

"Church?" she asked. Her voice carried more derision than she'd intended.

"I know, I know. It's like I just handed you every cliché in the book. Give it a chance, though. We accept everybody, regardless of their past. More than a few former addicts, and they've managed to clean themselves up."

"Meetings? Rehab?"

"No. It's just…a community. Maybe you'll like it, and maybe you'll decide it isn't your thing. Up to you. I'm just asking you to give it a shot. It might do you some good."

She turned the card back and forth, letting the stale fluorescents play off its surface. Some anonymous machine beeped in the distance. "What happens if I don't want to give it a shot?"

Officer Ruiz downed the rest of his coffee in a single pull. He dove into his wallet again, returned with a twenty, which he folded and handed to her as he climbed out of his chair. "Then you don't, but I think it would do you some good. You can use this for cab fare once you're released. Either way, take care of yourself, okay? You're young, Lizzie. It's nowhere near too late to turn things around. We can shed our pasts like old skin."

She took the bill from him and crumpled it into her pocket. When she looked up, Officer Ruiz was leaving the room. For a second, she stared at the ghost of his back. Then, she looked back to the card and started thinking.

THE CROWD FILTERING INTO the pavilion moved slower than she'd ever seen. Inspecting the crowd, she noticed terror and despair, both of which were new. Sure, in the past she'd seen things like fatigue and irritation, even genuine worry.

The ever more frequent drills had, at some point or another, rubbed almost everyone in the congregation the wrong way. Even then, there had been a sense of resolution lining those faces. *We do this to get better, so we can be our best. This is something we do so we're ready in case the time comes one day.* Now that the time had come, she found a congregation resolved not to perform but surrender.

The thought took her mind back to Mrs. Winters, the desperate words she'd said as she held a shivering Reggie at her side. *Everyone will have to drink no matter what.*

She wanted to believe that wasn't true, that the process the community had agreed upon would be upheld. It had only been twenty minutes, though. If Reverend Shaw wouldn't give them the full hour he'd promised, what else would he refuse to give?

As they reached the pavilion's edge, she located Walter and Stan. Instead of the jovial pair she'd seen only thirty minutes before, she found the two friends bickering.

Walter placed his hands on his friend's shoulder. "Calm down. You don't know that."

"I know bullshit when I smell it. Don't try to tell me what I know and what I don't." His face was red, anger forming hard creases. "It's from a movie, okay? I've heard it before, and it's from a goddamn movie!"

Stan had never cursed before, not that she'd heard. Elizabeth took a step in their direction, but then Carlos touched her shoulder. "We don't need the attention."

She swallowed hard. Of course, he was right. The best course of action was to go with the flow, keep quiet and as out of sight as possible.

Why am I so afraid? she thought. *I believe in this. I believe in all of this. There's nothing to be afraid of except what might be on the other side of the jungle.*

You don't believe that anymore, do you? You have doubts.

Shut up. I do believe.

Her hand in Carlos's, she sat down on one of the benches. Around her, the murmuring crowd reminded her of bees. She breathed deep and tried to pick up snatches of conversation, but it was all a drone, hundreds of voices mashing together into white noise. Instead of another attempt, she tried to concentrate on Reggie and his aunt. As long as guards didn't make a sweep of the cabins, they could easily go unnoticed. If Tommy took some men and went looking, however...

Scanning the crowd for Reverend Shaw's right hand, she felt doubt creep back in. No, it wasn't creeping. The awful emotion was pounding on her brain with a battering ram, demanding entry. Why would the reverend send guards to look for people who were hiding? That wasn't free will, that was a hunt. He'd already sent men with guns into the jungle.

To protect us. There are monsters in the world.

Are there really?

Shut up!

When she finally found Tommy, he stood at the door to Reverend Shaw's cabin. Arms crossed, he almost looked like he had in the emergency room more than a year prior. The gun on his hip helped, as did the way he swept his gaze back and forth over Sunrise Gardens. She wondered how many of his cop instincts remained. Probably all of them. Why else would Shaw keep him so close?

A frown tried to form on her face, but she fought it off. Despite her doubts and internal accusations, the reverend and his congregation had saved her, rebuilt her into a stronger and better person. To doubt was betrayal.

The door to Shaw's cabin opened, and the man stepped out, once again with Rita on his arm. He wiped a hand across his nose as he nodded to Tommy, and together the trio approached the pavilion.

Was the reverend using? No. Impossible. The jungle, after all, was full of things to which their immune systems were just now growing accustomed. Some bug or allergy wasn't an impossibility. She knew the signs, though, had seen them in kitchens and clubs and bathroom stalls. Was he really on drugs?

Elizabeth breathed deep and tried to fight off the dizziness and nausea that rioted through her body. It was too much, just way too much. She fought to cling to her faith, but it kept cracking, breaking into pieces and falling through her fingers. With will and desperation, she struggled to force it back together. *I chose this*, she thought. *I believe in this. It saved me.*

Save yourself, another voice told her.

As Reverend Shaw approached the pavilion, he again smiled and waved, a celebrity greeting his fans, but this time the cheers he received blended with shouts of anger and confusion. The hive buzz only grew as the reverend and his inner circle approached. By the time he stepped up to his pulpit, the sound had grown to something just shy of a roar. Shaw held up his hands for quiet, and the noise shriveled some, but a low, nervous rumble persisted.

"I understand," he said. "Believe me, friends, I understand. These are trying times, frightening times. What we find ourselves confronted with, it is a greater threat than anything we have previously faced. As a community, however, we are strong. I look out on you, and I see the strongest people I've ever encountered. I believe in you, and I am thankful for you. What we have to do, I know we'll accomplish."

Everyone will have to drink no matter what.

She squeezed Carlos's hand tighter. He reached over to rub her arm. Together, they could face this. They could face anything, she knew.

"Port Savoi!" somebody shouted. "They need to come back!"

Reverend Shaw nodded. "Yes, we still have people in Port Savoi. I sent men to bring them home, but the monsters have already reached the town. It is my sincere hope that the men I sent can bring our people home, but I can't make any promises."

"Why are we meeting early?"

"I'd hoped we would have more time, that the apocalypse was not right on our doorstep, but Port Savoi is only a short few hours away, which means the monsters could already be nearby. Discussion…I won't lie; I expect discussion to take some time. We need to make our decision before the demons crash through our gates and sweep over us like the great flood, itself. What we need to do is build our own ark. Yes, it is a terrible ark, but these are terrible times.

"I ask you this: do you want to watch the dead feast upon your loved ones? Upon your children? Do you want to risk coming back to be the one that murders your family? No, I don't believe any of you good people do. There's only one way to stop such sacrilege. What we choose to do, it's the right way. We…it paralyzes the nervous system so we cannot rise again. Really, it's that simple.

"I know, I know. This decision, it is horrible, and it is difficult. It may be the most difficult decision you'll–we'll–ever make, but it is the right decision. We will choose our end so that our end does not choose us. This is the way God wants it. This is why He gave us free will."

The rumble following his words was more positive than the previous one. Elizabeth heard exalted "Amens!" pierce the air. People applauded. The reverend's words did make sense. If what was happening outside Sunrise Gardens was real, of course paralyzing the nervous system would keep them from killing each other. Still…

"We can defend ourselves!" somebody said. She couldn't spot the speaker in the crowd, but a good portion of the congregation applauded.

Reverend Shaw held up his hands. He nodded like a father needing to explain things to a confused child. "I know it seems that way. If God gave us free will, why can't we use that to fight? We could be the white knights of this world, making a last stand against the demons of Hell just as we made a stand against the oppression of tyranny. Perhaps we could even survive. One day, we may even be able to rebuild civilization, create this Earth into the Paradise we hoped to one day birth through love and charity.

"We mustn't fool ourselves, though. These sorts of fantasies are just that: fantasy. To attempt these things is certainly a path full of pain and sorrow and horror. As Christians, we need not suffer needlessly. To do so is to spit in the face of God. What we do here today, it is the courageous choice. It is our way of praising God and to say, 'We love you, and we will not allow our flesh to be sustenance to the demons of Hell.' We here, we love God and

His Word. I know each of you love Him as much as I do. Make no mistake, to let our flesh become their bread is the highest form of sacrilege. To survive is to sin, and it is the gravest sin we can make."

The applause was a roar. It drowned out the dissenters, and Elizabeth's fear swelled even as she felt a strange bolstering of her courage. Reverend Shaw spoke the reality of things, same as he always had, as the knowledge that she was doing the right thing filled her with bravery that bordered on pride. Still, Mrs. Winters' words chipped at her brain, a chisel against stone.

What if it was all a play? The reverend could be working on their fears—on their pride—controlling them in the best way he knew how, by letting every last one of them believe they were special. All over, people cheated others by doing the same thing. The number of marks didn't matter, just the result.

Elizabeth was still trying to decide which she really believed when Carlos stood, his hand still wrapping hers, and waved. "Reverend Shaw! Reverend Shaw!" His voice rang with an excitement that sounded almost desperate.

"Yes, Son," the reverend said. His smile was warm, understanding.

She felt a tug at her hand, and it brought a smile to her face. In all the fear and confusion and anxiety, she'd almost forgotten their plan. As she stood, her eyes drifted to Carlos. His gaze met hers for a second, and it washed away the fear, the thoughts of Reggie and his aunt hiding in her cabin, everything. She loved him, and he loved her. Together, she felt as though they could conquer the entire world. At the very least, she could face whatever sliver of future remained if she had him by her side.

"I'm Carlos Ruiz, and this is Elizabeth Daniels," he said.

"I know Elizabeth. She's done an amazing job teaching the children of Sunrise Gardens."

A round of applause rose through the pavilion, and Elizabeth felt her face grow hot. Carlos gave her hand an extra squeeze. She hoped her smile didn't look embarrassed.

"What is your concern, Carlos?" Reverend Shaw asked.

"It's not really a concern, Father. Elizabeth and I, we've... we're in love."

More applause. Elizabeth felt her face grow hotter still.

"Love is a good thing, Carlos. The grandest thing on God's Earth."

"Yes, Father. We were...well, we know what the Gardens faces is...it's terrible. While we understand the need for discussion—really, we do—and will go along with whatever the congregation decides, we were hoping...wow, this is..."

The reverend shook his head, came up smiling. "I understand, Carlos. Please, continue. We have important matters to attend to."

Elizabeth felt sweat against her hand. She rubbed her thumb against Carlos's skin, hoping it might give him strength.

"Right," Carlos said. "Like I said, we're in love. We want to spend the rest of our lives together. So, we were hoping that maybe before discussion, or at least before, well, you know, whatever decision is made, that you might do us the honor of marrying us."

The congregation erupted in cheers, a sound so overwhelming Elizabeth felt her knees begin to buckle. She wrapped both arms around Carlos and hugged him tight. He responded with a kiss to her forehead, and she looked up and pulled him to her, pressing her lips to his. The cheering swelled, a crescendo she felt in her very core. It warmed her like fire, swept her along so that, for the first time since Mrs. Winters had appeared on her doorstep, she thought, *This is right. This is what I want. I belong here with these people, and I'll die here with these people. And that's okay.*

Slowly, she turned her eyes from Carlos and back to the reverend. Around them, the congregation's applause flowed and ebbed, waves crashing. The combination of the joy around her and the joy within her filled her so thoroughly that it took several moments to realize Reverend Shaw wasn't clapping along with everyone else. He didn't smile. If anything, his expression conveyed annoyance, anger. His jaw clenched, the flesh there quivering the slightest bit. Shadows grew around his eyes, and his lips twisted into a sneer when he sniffed hard and wiped the back of his hand under his nose. Slowly, her joy became apprehension, became embarrassment. Carlos put an arm around her shoulders and squeezed her, but her eyes remained locked on the reverend's.

"You're more important than our community. Is that what you think?" Reverend Shaw said.

"What?" Carlos asked. "No. Father, we're—"

"You're children. Further, one of you is a great teacher, and the other is a pack mule. You don't belong together, and you're both too naïve to realize it."

Elizabeth felt her face grow slack even as she felt Carlos stiffen at her side. Had he really said that? Could he really mean it?

"Right now, here, when the world is collapsing on itself to make way for chaos, you think being together is what you want," he said. "It is the most important thing in your lives, the thing which will complete you, make you whole. Surely, you think your pathetic, childish infatuation will keep all the demons of Hell at bay! Do you want to rut while we watch, too? 'Marry us, Reverend Shaw! Our Bread and Circuses will keep the dead people from eating our flesh!' Well, I'm not fooled. These good people, when they really think about it, are not fooled. They see through your idiocy. They see through your immaturity. As the world ends, we must hold fast to the teachings of our beloved God, and we must not forsake him, and these wonderful people will not allow you to do so!"

The applause had died, a heavy silence replacing it. When Elizabeth swallowed, the nervous action crackled in her ears. This couldn't be happening. How could this really be happening?

Reverend Shaw pounded a fist against his pulpit. His face flared red with anger. "Teachers cannot love mules! She is a mind and a heart, and you are a machine and a tool. You are incapable of loving each other! Were the world to continue, we would select mates for you, and you would breed for the betterment of Sunrise Gardens. You *do not* get to decide you are more important than the whole!

"You're selfish!" His finger jabbed at them, then traveled from one side of the pavilion to the other. "You put yourselves, your idiot animal urges, before everyone else here. You spit in the face of God. We should stop discussion while wolves creep ever closer to our door, so you can feel better about your filthy sin. Did you think these good people wouldn't see the truth of things? Do you believe they're blind and dumb? We are under attack! Hell has opened up, and it threatens to swallow Sunrise Gardens and everyone here, but you don't care!"

"That's...that's not true," Carlos said. His voice was small, though. Elizabeth barely heard it over the awful quiet. Slowly, a smattering of boos and jeers lifted up from the congregation, and then more followed in their wake. If anyone still backed their union, their voices disappeared beneath the din.

"You hear them," Reverend Shaw said. "Everyone hates you for your selfishness, for your sin. You thought yourselves better than this community, better than God, and now everyone sees the truth of your ways."

Elizabeth watched as angry faces turned toward them. She saw glares and sneers, saw curses form on lips. A man she didn't recognize spat at them. Shrinking against Carlos, she wondered how a crowd could turn so quickly. Seconds before, the congregation had cheered them. Now, she felt genuine terror riot through her system. When she thought of Mrs. Winters and Reggie hiding in her cabin, she wished she could be with them. Anything had to be better than this.

"Separate them."

She almost didn't hear the words, but they found her in the second before she saw those closest grab at their arms. Twisting, she wrenched free, tried to cling to Carlos, but he already had several sets of hands on him. They dragged him off his feet, and he almost spilled to the pavilion floor. Shouting, he stretched an arm toward her, and she screamed as she lunged for his hand.

Carlos threw a punch. She didn't see it land, but she heard the meaty smack of his knuckles against flesh, heard the groan as a body sagged toward the floor. He cocked back to swing again, but she lost sight of him among the tide of bodies that rushed between them. Thrashing and bucking, trying to draw breath for another cry, she fought against it, but something caught her ankle, and her balance disappeared in a sudden lurch of gravity. A hand cracked

across her cheek, and then a heavy fist slammed into her belly. Her breath disappeared in an explosion of air, and a clucking series of croaks replaced it. All of her limbs sagged, then, and the crowd carried her away.

A piercing scream froze everything. The hands on Elizabeth stopped dragging and hitting her. The rumble of angry voices collapsed to nothing. Even her gasps gave way to frightened breaths. Suspended in the grip of seven others, she looked around for the scream's source with wild eyes.

Then, the scream came again.

"They're here!"

SHE SPENT THREE WEEKS with the card the police officer had handed her. When working, she kept it in her back pocket, whipping it out on occasion to inspect the gold letters. She ran her fingertips over it as she sat in her apartment, numb with alcohol.

It always ended the same way: a memory of the patrolman's words, comforting and supportive, echoing in her ears before she frowned and tucked the card back in her pocket. Over and over, she considered tossing it. Church wasn't going to fix her problems. She kept it, though, turning over the thick paper, feeling the lettering beneath her fingertips. Each time, she held it a little longer, noticed some new detail in its surface, a scratch or buffed spot. Maybe it was normal wear and tear, but maybe it was simple discovery, her senses discovering more and more mysteries inside a rectangle of hard paper.

She found herself once again examining the card as the sun rose on Sunday morning. No sleep, dizzy and sloppy. She staggered from the bathroom, her balance little more than a memory. Her stomach twisted, and her head pounded, a hangover arriving before she'd even sobered up.

"Goddammit." She sneered at herself, unable to find the joy in her drunk. Everything felt heavy, distant. Another beer didn't help. Leaning back on her couch, she waited for the booze to drown her headache, but it didn't happen.

Her eyes felt hot, wet. She slapped a hand across her face. As she struck herself a second time, she wondered if she was trying to bring herself back to reality or punish herself. Maybe it didn't matter.

When she blinked the tears from her eyes, she found the rest of the beer waiting for her on the cheap coffee table she'd found on a curb months before. She imagined it was watching her, daring her to try to pour it down the sink. *I control you, Lizzie,* it said. *Don't bother fighting it. You know it's true.*

"Shut up." Her voice was barely a whimper. The first sob followed, hard and painful, and then the tears spilled down her cheeks.

"I can't do this. I can't do this anymore." She knew the words were the truth. Even as she leaned forward and sucked down the can's remains, hating herself more than she thought possible, she knew she'd reached bottom, landed hard and heavy. She balled her hand into a fist and brought it down hard on the table. Only the slightest twinge of pain registered, but she knew it would hurt like hell later. She knew the phenomenon well, had woken a day later decorated with scrapes and bruises from accidents she couldn't recall. It had happened more times than she could count.

Maybe she could kill herself. It would solve more than a few problems.

"Hell with this. Just...*dammit!*" Groaning, she wiped her eyes with the heels of her hands and looked at the card again. The address looked blurry, but she could read it. Again and again, she spoke it out loud, committing it to memory.

"You're still drunk, idiot," she told herself, but it didn't matter. She'd be drunk the rest of the day, and she'd be miserable through all of it. Once she crashed, she'd feel even worse, and she didn't know what she might do to herself in that state. The time had come to admit she needed help.

Nodding, she stood from the couch, and tucked the card back into her pocket. Repeating the address to herself, she went to her bedroom to find some clean clothes.

SCREAMS AND SHOUTS ERUPTED around her, and the hands grasping at her fell away. She sensed movement, panicked bodies and a frightened rush. The tide shoved her back and forth, and she hit her hands and knees before fighting back to her feet.

Pushing against the throng, she searched for Carlos. She found him a dozen yards away, his arms pinned behind his back and a trio of men holding him in place. His gaze, somehow angry and frightened at once, fixed on something beyond the pavilion. She followed it past the crowd and past Reverend Shaw, who shouted into the microphone for calm, to the jungle's edge. Her doubts vanished and everything went numb, her legs threatening to spill her back to the floor.

Two of them lurched across the field, heading for the pavilion and the congregation inside. Arms jerking, backs bucking, their movements revealed only the slightest facsimile of humanity. Animalistic violence had taken its place. When the crowd slowly fell silent and pushed toward the pavilion's rear edge, Elizabeth heard the dead men's rasping breath.

"Tommy," the reverend said, and his right hand drew his pistol and marched toward the creatures.

The congregation held their breath as though they were a single body. Tommy approached the cannibals with calm, purposeful steps. He kept his weapon at his side, gripped with both hands. For a moment, the sound of rasping breath and the whisper of Tommy's feet through the tall grass became a strange, hushed chorus ringing through Sunrise Garden.

Tommy dropped to one knee when the monsters came within maybe fifty yards. Elizabeth watched as his shoulders rolled and he raised the pistol, aimed.

A cracking shot split the quiet. One of the cannibals' heads snapped backward, red mist shooting from the back of its head, and then it dropped, the percussive thump of its body against the ground putting an exclamation point on things. The other turned, standing up straight and looking at its fallen companion. A second shot rang out, and it fell, too. Silence returned to Sunrise Gardens.

Elizabeth exhaled. She felt suddenly exhausted, and she realized she'd been tensing every last one of her muscles. Struggling against the weakness sewn through her entire body, she looked to Carlos. His eyes held hers for a second, and then she rushed toward him. She managed a trio of steps before the hands returned,

holding her fast. There was no yelling this time, no chaos, just fingers like iron restraints on her arms. Across the pavilion, Carlos struggled to break free of his captors but failed.

"You see what we're up against," Reverend Shaw said. "I know times like these test the faith of even the strongest men, but trust your eyes. The demons wait at our doorstep. More will come, and they will crash over us like waves."

A fresh murmur rippled through the congregation. Elizabeth saw frightened faces, was sure she wore one herself.

"If anyone wants to discuss our decision, I'll allow it," Shaw said. Tommy returned to his side, pistol still in hand. "I implore you, though—I beg you—do not let us waste time. The drink is ready. We can be in Heaven before the demons even arrive. By destroying our bodies, we will save our souls from defilement. Line up, please. Our time is running out. We need to do this before Hell crashes through our gates."

Slowly, the congregation started moving. One by one, they made their way toward the table of plastic buckets and metal pails. Elizabeth felt the hands fall away from her. If anyone still cared what she did, they didn't show it. They'd become cattle wandering toward the trough, their expressions resigned but determined.

She moved against the tide, slipping between bodies until she found herself at Carlos' side again.

"Thank God," he said, throwing his arms around her. She squeezed him with all the strength she could muster. "What do we do?"

"I'm not sure." She hated that the truth was so disappointing to her.

"Maybe we should go," he said. "We aren't wanted here."

"Right." Even watching Tommy drop the pair of monsters hadn't shaken Reverend Shaw's words from her mind. *A teacher and a pack mule.* What had happened to all his talk about equality? She thought of politicians and their back and forth, twisting their opinions when it suited them. For so long now, she'd thought the reverend was different, that he really wanted to create a kind of paradise on Earth. Now, she saw the truth of things, and it left her feeling hollow and bitter.

"C'mon." Carlos took her hand and started pulling her toward the pavilion's edge. As they picked up speed, she thought of Reggie. They'd need to collect him and his aunt. Yes, she might slow them down, but she refused to abandon the woman who'd started opening her eyes. She owed her a chance at survival, no matter how slim.

Carlos froze, and she almost moved past him before she realized what was happening. Guards had closed around the pavilion's perimeter. From where she stood, she saw three of them, each armed with a rifle. They scanned the crowd, searching for problems. Breathing deep, fighting to appear calm, she pulled Carlos back into the crowd.

"This is insane," she said. He only nodded.

A choking gasp sliced through the pavilion. Elizabeth jumped, sure another monster had arrived. Instead, she saw a woman stagger away from the table full of buckets and pails. With one hand, she clawed at her throat. The other hand spasmed, dropping a paper cup into the grass. She lurched with each step. Her mouth gaped and snapped shut, and her eyes grew wider as she turned and looked to the congregation. With one hand, she reached out, almost pleading, and then she fell to the ground, still.

She wanted to believe seeing the first death would shock the rest of the congregation to their senses. Surely, no one could watch such an awful thing and then willingly follow. The man behind her took his paper cup and knocked back its contents in a single belt, though. He moved quickly, making nearly ten yards before his body started jerking.

"What's wrong with you all?" a voice said. "Can't you see this is horseshit?"

Before she saw Walter, she recognized his voice. When she found him, he was approaching the pulpit, fists shaking at his sides. For a moment, his eyes locked on Reverend Shaw's. The pair faced off. Around them, the air hung still. Only the sound of liquid pouring into paper cups, of people gasping and choking in the grass, broke the silence.

Walter wheeled on the shuffling crowd. "He's making this up!"

"You saw them!" a voice replied.

"And I saw them die before they got anywhere close to us! You all saw it!" He threw a hand toward the reverend. "He's talking out his ass! Those news reports came from fucking movies! He's just throwing together ideas and hoping not a single one of you can think for yourselves. Goddammit, can't you tell he's making this up as—"

The side of Walter's head exploded before he could finish his thought. Blood and bone turned to mist and splinters, and his body dropped the same as the pair of monsters had moments before. Someone gasped, but no cries or shouts filled the pavilion. Instead, a silence like weight hung over everything.

Tommy stood, pistol at the end of his outstretched arm, and grimaced. Blood flecked his face. As he lowered the weapon to his side, he wiped his mouth with his free hand, smearing crimson across his skin.

"There you have it," Reverend Shaw said. His voice crackled across the congregation. "You are a believer, or you are an abomination. We can no longer tolerate abominations. You will drink, or we will baptize you with lead. So sayeth the Lord."

Elizabeth found Stan among the crowd. She saw tears on his face, his mouth opening and closing soundlessly. Maybe he was looking at Tommy, or maybe he was looking at the reverend. She couldn't tell. For all she knew, he could be staring at nothing. How does a person handle the cold blooded murder of their best friend? When his face crumpled into sadness and he shuffled toward the line that led to the buckets and pails, Elizabeth knew.

A hand tightened like iron around her wrist, and she almost screamed before she realized it was Carlos. "C'mon," he said, yanking her toward the street.

Terrified, she looked for the guards. They'd moved closer to the crowd, beginning to herd the congregation. If nothing else, the sight slammed the truth full force into her brain, almost knocking her to her knees as it shattered the last of her faith. *Cattle,* she thought. *Nothing but cattle. It's all we ever were.*

"Quick. Quiet." Carlos spoke in whispers as he hugged the pavilions edge. He didn't have to drag her more than a few steps before she found her feet and kept pace with him, hugging the first wall they found and ducking out of sight.

"Jesus Christ," she said. Her pulse hammered in her ears. She could feel it pounding against the skin of her neck. From around the corner, she heard more choking, a single cry of agony. Reverend Shaw's voice crackled again.

"Drink," he said. "It's how God wants us to save ourselves."

"Reggie," she said.

Carlos gave her a single nod. "I know."

Ducking low, they darted from cabin to cabin, fighting the mud that dragged at their feet. Behind them, the sounds of death continued to rise as a single, horrible choir. Another shot rang out, and she almost dove out of reflex before she realized it was someone else getting their final ticket punched. She wondered if it was Stan joining his best friend.

They reached her cabin, and she threw a glance over her shoulder. The street appeared clear. As quick as she could, she shoved the door open and jerked Carlos inside.

"No!" Reggie's voice was shrill, terrified.

Elizabeth held a finger to her lips, and Reggie nodded.

"It's started?" Mrs. Winters asked.

"Yeah."

"We're going," Carlos said. "Now."

Mrs. Winters kissed her nephew's head. "Take him," she said.

"We're taking both of you," Elizabeth said. "Come on."

"Just take Reggie. I'll only hold you up."

She dropped into a crouch in front of the pair. A single breath quelled some of the fear. In its place rose the things she still chose to believe. On one knee, she thought of Walter's anger and Stan's sadness. She thought of herself on a sidewalk in Kissimme, crying and then slamming her head into a light post. Her thoughts shifted to the strength it had taken to get sober, to believe in something greater than booze. Finally, she thought about where she realized her strength really lied, what she really believed in: herself.

"This is not a discussion," she said. "Stand up now. We're going."

Slowly, Mrs. Winters nodded. She squeezed Reggie's hand. "Can you be brave for me?" she asked.

"Yes."

"Good. Elizabeth is going to take us to safety."

"That's right. I am." For an instant, she registered the shock that she really did believe her words. They sounded foolish, brazen, but she felt every syllable in her heart, and she intended to make them the truth. She'd been fooled again, Reverend Shaw just being another high to replace the old one. Knowing the truth pissed her off, and she knew the time had come to throw off that last shackle.

She looked to Carlos. "Is it clear?"

"Yeah." He gave a second glance through the window. "Don't know for how long."

"So we go. Everybody stay quiet and move as fast as you can. We're heading for the jungle."

"Lizzie…" Carlos let her name hang in the air, and she knew what he meant. Men with guns. He'd seen them leave in the trucks almost an hour before.

"So we stay *really* quiet."

"Okay."

"All right. Let's go."

Elizabeth led the group into the street. Even at a distance, the sound from the pavilion sent shivers through her. Agonized screams and gasps for breath filled the air. She let them stop her for a single instant. Rooted to the ground, she thought of the people she'd known and trusted, dying in pain because they believed.

Reggie pulled at her wrist. "Are those the monsters?"

"No, sweetie. That's something else."

She led the group down the boggy street. When they reached the next cabin, she hugged the structure's wall and crept to the edge. She peered around the corner, searching for guards. The path to the next structure—the classroom—looked clear, but she spent an extra second making sure. Holding her breath, she prayed they wouldn't hear gunfire erupt as soon as they stepped into the open. Then she chuckled as she realized she still saw a point in prayer.

Moving in a crouch, she darted into the open. Reggie clutched at her shirt with his free hand, and she hoped she wouldn't feel him drop to the ground. Every second counted. If bullets started piercing the air while they were all a tangle of limbs...

When she shoved her back to the classroom's wall and pulled Reggie tight against her side, she realized she'd been holding her breath. Carlos reached them with Mrs. Winters a second later.

"Two more buildings and then the jungle," he said. "What happens then?"

"I guess we stay close to the road," Elizabeth said. "Maybe we can flag down a truck. A friendly truck."

"And go where? Port Savoi? You heard Reverend Shaw. They're already—"

She slapped her hands over Reggie's ears and gave him a hard look. "We don't know how much he said is real." Even as she spoke, she thought of the two figures shuffling across the grass, their movements that were somehow both slow and spastic. If Port Savoi was full of such things—if they'd truly overrun the entire world—then they were only delaying their deaths, but Reggie didn't need to know that.

Or did he deserve to know the truth? Was hiding the facts of their situation any better than lying about them? Creeping along the classroom's wall, she decided she could figure it out once they were past the armed guards.

They crossed the school without incident and reached the infirmary. Elizabeth thought of how Marnie had loaded poison onto a cart inside those walls earlier that day. Had she experienced any doubts as she prepared to kill hundreds of believers? She wondered if, even before her faith had shattered, she could have performed such a task. Such a different job than teaching children, yet she'd always led the kids to the pavilion for drills, told them they were getting better so they could be their best. For the first time, she wondered which of the two was worse: the poisoner mixing a concoction or the pied piper who led the children to drink. Which one was the real murderer?

If anyone noticed her viciously shake her head as they neared the infirmary's corner, no one mentioned it. Maybe they heard the soft footsteps in tall grass before she did, or perhaps their own questions and worries distracted them. She only heard movement a split second before she peeked around the corner, hoping for a clear path to the jungle's edge.

Instead of empty grass, she saw one of the guards. His back was turned, but the rifle in his hands looked ready to go.

Elizabeth held a hand up to the others, then motioned with both hands, pointing an imaginary rifle. Carlos nodded, his face grave, and Mrs. Winters rested her hands on Reggie's shoulders. The boy shivered, and his lips trembled with the first signs of panic. Trying to keep her expression calm, Elizabeth held a finger to her lips, asking Reggie a question with her eyes. When he nodded, she hoped they truly were on the same page.

A shrug from Carlos asked her what they should do. Her back pressed against the infirmary, she wondered the same thing. If they tried to go back, the guard might hear them. If they broke for the jungle, he almost certainly would. Perhaps they could wait for him to wander off, but they were already exposed. They couldn't risk standing still.

She caught the look from Mrs. Winters, eyes hard and determined, and shook her head. The woman's expression didn't change, just bore deeper into Elizabeth's mind. Breathing deep, she gave the woman a slow nod. It was their only chance, and she knew it.

Mrs. Winters lowered herself into a crouch and turned Reggie to face her. Slowly, she kissed the boy's forehead. The whisper she spoke to the boy was too low for Elizabeth to hear, but she read the words with ease. *Be quiet. Be careful. I love you.*

Reggie grabbed at his aunt's sleeve. He sucked in a sharp breath, preparing to cry out, but the woman placed a finger to his lips and shook her head, then snatched him up in a strong hug. Kissing his head once again. Elizabeth wiped away the tears blossoming in her eyes. She needed to be able to see when the time came.

Mrs. Winters stood. She fought back tears as she turned away from her nephew, and Carlos touched her arm, mouthed the words *Thank you.* She nodded and then walked past him, smoothing out her clothes as she walked away. Reggie made a desperate lunge for her, but Elizabeth caught him, snaking an arm around his waist and clamping her free hand over his mouth. He struggled as his aunt rounded the infirmary's corner and stepped into the street, but Elizabeth held him close, whispered into his ear.

"She's very brave," she said. "She's trying to save us. I need you to be brave, too. Okay?"

She felt him nod against her hand, then jumped as he heard the guard say, "Hey!"

"What do you want?" Distance muffled Mrs. Winters' voice, but Elizabeth understood it just fine.

"You're supposed to be at the pavilion. Everybody is."

"You ain't there."

Whispered footsteps trailed from the Gardens' border toward the street. "C'mon. You know how this works."

"What's happening at the pavilion?"

"You been asleep or something?"

"Yeah. Just woke up and couldn't find anybody around."

Keeping her hand tight over Reggie's mouth, Elizabeth looked around the corner again. The guard had disappeared. Her breath came a little faster as she realized their opportunity had come, that they might not get another chance.

Her first step felt almost impossible. She held her breath to keep from screaming, her teeth grinding, and pulled Reggie behind her. Moving with quick steps, she fought to stay silent. The sound of grass brushing across her ankles and calves seemed impossibly loud, spiking her fear. Even the continuing conversation behind her provided only the slightest measure of relief.

"Go to the pavilion, please. It's mandatory."

"Mandatory? Jesus, are we having another drill?"

"Ma'am, just head to the pavilion."

"I'll get to it. I'm going to take a little walk first."

Ten yards from cover, Elizabeth finally took a breath. Nervous stars burned in her vision. She wanted to make a break for it, just take off at a sprint and crash through the foliage, but she fought the temptation. Behind her, the guard said something she couldn't make out. Mrs. Winters answered with a shout.

"How about you tell the reverend to kiss my old ass?"

Then, she reached the border and pushed through, pulling Reggie into the dense foliage and waiting for Carlos to join them before continuing. Only when enormous leaves blocked their view of Sunrise Gardens did she dare move faster.

More shouts rose up, the guard and Reggie's aunt arguing in the street, but the words had become an angry mash. She'd led their trio maybe twenty yards when the shot rang out.

"Thank you, Mrs. Winters." she whispered.

THE JUNGLE SWALLOWED ALL sound but their careful foot-steps. No more gunshots cut the air, and the sounds of choking death disappeared. Fifty yards into the thick foliage, they felt iso-lated, alone.

Elizabeth closed her eyes and slumped to the ground. She knew they needed to keep moving, but which way? Fleeing in ter-ror, it turned out, was a lot different than leaving with a plan. Dammit, they hadn't even packed any food. Maybe they could forage as they made their way to Port Savoi. She just wanted a minute to think.

"We should keep going," Carlos said.

Right. She'd have to think on her feet.

"Is she coming?" Reggie asked.

"Huh?" she said.

"My aunt."

She clamped her eyes shut and steeled her thoughts. As much as she hated it, she couldn't deal with Reggie's question yet. "Let's keep going," she said. Carlos nodded, and she took the boy's hand and marched deeper into the jungle.

HER LEGS FROZE HALFWAY up the church steps. Already, she heard the sound of an organ seeping through the doors, its notes regal and joyous. That meant they'd already started, which meant when she entered they'd look. All of them. Dozens of heads—maybe hundreds—turning to see who'd dared to be late. She couldn't face that. It was too much.

She could go back to her apartment, maybe sleep off her bender. Or grab another bottle of vodka. It was easier, for sure, and better than the beer she'd finished off. Curling her trembling hands into hard fists, she thought about pouring cold vodka into a clean glass.

"Fuck you, Lizzie," she said. "Not anymore."

Teeth grinding, she continued her climb. She felt heavier with each step, but she fought through it, her eyes fixed on the church doors' large, ornate handles. When she finally reached the doors and took hold, she felt exhausted and out of breath. Her legs wobbled, and her knees threatened to buckle, so she bit down hard on her lips. Pain lanced her jaw, and the taste of blood brought her back to her senses.

"Here goes nothing."

She opened the heavy door, the organ's music washed over her like a rolling tide.

ELIZABETH ALMOST STUMBLED INTO the guards before she heard them. Laughter and voices stopped her cold, and she motioned for Carlos and Reggie to do the same. Her fear spiked. Had the guards heard their footsteps?

Peering through the foliage, she saw the quartet standing less than ten yards away, rifles slung over their shoulders and hand-guns on their hips. She fixated on their weapons a moment, her stomach turning as she thought the reverend really had sent his men into the jungle to kill anyone who might try to leave, but then she realized what the guards were doing, and her insides roiled.

One of the pair worked on the other, with sponges and their fingertips, applying makeup to the men, giving them shadowed, hollow eyes and rotten skin. Blood that had to be fake marred their clothes, which had been torn far too thoroughly for the damage to be normal wear and tear. As she watched, Reggie and Carlos at her back, one of the guards spoke to his makeup artist.

"Make it look good, right? I'm supposed to be dead."

"You look as dead as I can make you. I'm not exactly an expert, here."

A third spoke up. "It's fine. You heard Tommy. He'll fire off his blanks before we even get close. It doesn't need to be a masterpiece."

Blanks? Elizabeth thought about when Tommy had killed the first two figures to lurch out of the jungle. Hadn't she seen a red spray when the first was hit? Maybe the reverend had set up a few guards with elaborate effects, or maybe Tommy wasn't working with blanks at all. For a second, she thought about warning the men, but then she realized the thought was foolish. They'd either kill her or march her right back to the pavilion. Besides, if they willingly helped Reverend Shaw with his charade, they deserved everything they got.

"Turn around slow."

Reggie screamed behind her, amplifying the sudden rush of terror that surged through her. She heard the quick rattle of a rifle jamming against a shoulder, and then she knew for certain another guard stood behind them. As she turned to see the man and his weapon, Carlos with his hands in the air, her fear gave way to a sinking weight. There would be no other escape. They'd lost.

Reggie screamed again, cowering against the ground. "No!"

"Shut up," the guard said. His face had been painted into a clumsy attempt at a corpse mask. Fake blood stained his shirt and bare arms.

"Liars." The word jabbed from Elizabeth's lips like a snake's tongue. "You're all fucking liars."

"Told you to shut up."

Behind her, Elizabeth heard heavy footsteps through the brush. The remaining guards.

At her feet, Reggie shook, head snapping back and forth. "Don't! Don't!" She reached down to comfort him, and the guard shook his weapon at her.

"Did I say to move, girl?"

Then she recognized the man. Even through the makeup job, she made out the face of Jason Murphy. Eyes she used to think of as fun and kind had turned mean, anxious.

"Jason," she said. "It's me, Elizabeth. You know me, right? The teacher? Caleb's in my class."

"Shut up."

"What are we supposed to do with them?" another guard asked.

"Walk them back."

"Like this?"

"Dammit."

She lifted her hands in surrender, looking Jason dead in the eye. "Where's Caleb? Where's Allison, Jason? Your wife. Did she drink? Did she make him drink?"

"I told you to shut up, dammit."

"Are you supposed to drink after this? Do you know why?" She caught a look from Carlos, one that asked what she was doing, and she realized she had no clue. Maybe she hoped to talk their way out of death, or maybe she just wanted to understand. No matter the reason, the words kept coming. "Can you tell me why?" she asked. "Seriously, I want to know, because I look at this, and I can tell it was a lie."

"The reverend played us the reports," he said.

"So why are you out here? Why are you dressed like this? Jesus Christ, why do you have guns? Maybe if you were supposed to defend The Gardens, I could get it, but you're keeping us in. You're painted up like monsters! We all know the rules, Jason! All of you do! It's supposed to be a choice!"

Elizabeth thought she saw hesitation in his eyes, the same doubt that had crept into her so recently. His mouth drew into a tight line, and she wondered if he was thinking of his wife.

"Forget this," a voice behind her said. "Just drop them."

Everything happened so fast. Reggie screamed something else, a high pitched squeal of a syllable she couldn't make out, and then Carlos dove for Jason. His bulk knocked the guard back before he could swing his weapon around, and the pair crashed into the underbrush. Reggie sprang to his feet in the same instant and ran. A pair of shots rang out, deafening Elizabeth, and she saw bark fly from a nearby tree, a giant leaf split violently, and then Reggie disappeared into the jungle.

Another trio of shots cracked through the air, snapping her attention away from the fleeing boy. She threw herself against the closest guard, sending his next shot wide, and scrambled for his rifle. One more shot pierced the sky, and then she froze as she felt the muzzle of a gun pressed to the back of her head.

"Get up," a voice said. "Do it slow."

Again, she lifted her hands. Her breath came in a ragged, gasping chain. This was it. They were going to kill her. They were going to kill…

Two of the guards approached Carlos and Jason. When she saw the pair of blossoming red stains on the back of her fiancé's shirt, a sob caught in her throat, refusing to leave until one of the men rolled him off Jason like a bag of grain. For an instant that felt like days, she could only stare at his face. His expression was somehow both pained and peaceful, but she found nothing there that would let her pretend he was still alive.

"What about the kid?" somebody asked.

"Doesn't matter."

And it didn't. Elizabeth knew that. Cold reality washing over her, she no longer cared what happened to her. It just didn't matter.

"Do it," she said. She closed her eyes, breathed deep. The air tasted rotten.

"What's that?"

"Just do it. Finish it. Hell if I care anymore."

"Help…"

The choking voice opened her eyes again, and she saw Jason. He clutched a hand to a wound in his side, but blood seeped through his fingers. Pain pinched his face, and his breath came in violent gasps.

"Dammit." One of the guards left her side to crouch over Jason. One hand on his chest, he muttered something she couldn't make out. An apology, maybe.

"Please," Jason said. With his free hand, he clutched at the guard's sleeve. "I don't…I don't want to come back. Let me go… go to Heaven."

The guard nodded. "You're a good man, Jason Murphy. A good Christian." He stood, knocking his rifle into his shoulder. "Do you want to pray?"

"Yeah."

Silence fell on the group, and Elizabeth considered running. Maybe she could chase Reggie and make sure he was okay, but a hand clamped around her wrist before she could reach a decision. She looked at the guard, hoping to recognize him, but instead found a stranger shaking his head at her, his eyes a warning.

A rifle shot shattered the moment, snapping her attention back to where Carlos and Jason lay. Again, the guard crouched, smoothing back the hair above Jason's ruined face. "Go be with your wife," he said.

"What about Carlos?" she asked.

"What do you mean?" The guard stood and returned to her, slinging the rifle over his shoulder.

"Carlos. Do you have to keep him from getting back up?" She tried to tell herself it wouldn't happen, but she couldn't be sure. More than anything, she wanted to know the man she loved wouldn't languish. She wanted him to go to Heaven with Mrs. Winters and the rest.

The remaining guards shared looks before considering Carlos's body. Finally, one of them spoke.

"Heretic."

Elizabeth watched, stunned by her anger, as the guard kicked Carlos hard in the ribs and then turned away. She considered attacking the men. At least they'd send her to be with the man she loved but the squawking of a walkie-talkie chopped down her thoughts.

"It's Tommy. Come in."

"Here."

"I heard shots. Everything okay out there?"

The guard eyed Elizabeth and then Carlos before peering in the direction Reggie had fled. For a second, his face screwed up in thought, and then he spoke. "Found a couple trying to walk out. One's down, and the other's with us. Murphy's down, too."

"Murphy?" Tommy asked.

"Yeah."

"All right. Bring the survivor on back. Everybody else come back, too."

"You don't need us to send another one or two toward the pavilion first?"

"No, it's done. Let's wrap it up."

Done. The word sounded so final, a period at the end of Sunrise Gardens' story. Elizabeth turned it over in her mind, thought about the four guards surrounding her, and admitted her story was almost finished, too. She hoped Reggie might survive, but she didn't like his chances. Monsters or not, he was a boy alone in the jungle.

One of the guards unholstered his pistol and stepped over Carlos. Without fanfare, he planted a bullet in his forehead. When he turned around, he shrugged.

"We're Christians. Mercy."

"Amen," a voice over Elizabeth's shoulder said.

She said it, too, the taste of tears salty on her tongue. "Amen."

THE QUARTET OF ARMED guards surrounded her, keeping her in the middle of a protective box. As they stepped free of the jungle and back into Sunrise Gardens, Elizabeth felt her breath catch hard in her throat. Her legs froze, and she didn't start walking again until one of the guards grabbed her by the elbow and shoved her forward.

Bodies. So many bodies. Hundreds of them lay clustered around the pavilion, tangled heaps of twisted limbs and awkwardly bent necks. She thought she could already hear the static drone of flies in the air. As they drew closer, she tried to remember how many people had relocated to Sunrise Gardens. Hundreds, at least. Maybe a thousand. So many people, so many lives, now discarded like garbage, piles of flesh left to rot in the sun.

A single figure walked among the bodies. Tommy. He walked with his hands on his hips, surveying the carnage around him. Elizabeth wondered where Reverend Shaw had gone.

Tommy stepped to the pulpit. A body sprawled behind it, and Elizabeth recognized the shirt before the reverend's right-hand man bent down and plucked a pistol from the corpse's grip. She felt her face twist into a disgusted smirk. So Reverend Shaw hadn't even found the courage to drink. Instead, he'd pulled a trigger and punched his ticket, chosen something sudden and painless. Reaching the pavilion, watching the guards consider the field of death around them, she found genuine hate for the reverend and what he'd done.

"So he was a coward, too," she said.

"Shut up, Lizzie." Tommy's voice didn't sound angry. It carried the flat note of business.

"My name's Elizabeth. I'm a teacher."

"Sure, you are."

"We can shed our pasts like old skin, right? You used to help people."

"I still do. Who have you helped?"

"As many as I could."

"Keep telling yourself that."

Elizabeth didn't bother trying to keep the hate from her eyes. "Keep pretending you're not a puppet. You're a…a…" She struggled for the right word, but it wouldn't come. Nothing felt sharp enough.

"Some teacher you turned out to be." He waved the remaining guards toward the metal pails waiting on the pavilion's far edge. "Go ahead. There's still enough left."

Without a word, the quartet left her. It occurred to her she should keep her eye on Tommy and his handgun, but she couldn't look away as the men wrestled their way through the sprawl of corpses, picked up their paper cups, and drank.

"It's not even real, is it?" she asked. The first gagging sounds reached her as she watched one of the guards stumble, clutching his throat, and then collapse to the ground.

"Of course it's real."

Elizabeth looked to Tommy and saw anger in his eyes, but she thought she might see doubt there, too. She set her jaw and refused to turn away as Tommy shook the handgun at her. "Look," she said, casting her arms wide.

"I can see." His eyes burned, rimmed with red and wet with tears.

"No one's waking up, Tommy. The dead aren't coming back."

"I know."

"He lied to us, Tommy."

"No, he didn't. He said…"

"That we wouldn't come back because we poisoned ourselves? Then why did they shoot Carlos in the head and say it was mercy? Why isn't there a hole in every skull here? They're not getting back up, Tommy. No one is. Anywhere. It was a goddamn lie."

"It wasn't!"

"You're not so sure, are you?"

"Shut up. I am."

His face told a different story. Eyes darting, he bit at his lip. A whimper escaped his throat.

"That thing you feel inside? That's your faith cracking," she said. "I felt the same thing when Shaw told me I wasn't allowed to marry Carlos. I felt it when he said we all have to die. Women, kids. Everybody. Did you feel it when you murdered Walter Redmond?"

Slowly, he surveyed the carnage around them. His face pinched hard, and she thought if the sound of four men dying didn't dominate the scene she might hear his teeth grinding. The pistol trembled in his fist.

"Dammit," he said.

"What's that?"

"Dammit!"

She saw the first tears cascade down his cheeks, and her heart broke for the man who meant to murder her, the man she'd watched murder so many others already. All of it done out of faith. So much time, their entire lives given over to faith, and that belief had only added up to a lie. If it wasn't so infuriating, it would almost be funny.

"State Department," he said. "I heard him say something about it a week ago before he started demanding time alone to listen to reports."

"They were coming here?"

"I don't know!" He pinched the bridge of his nose like he had a severe sinus headache. Twice, he stomped a foot on the pavilion floor. "I had to go to Port Savoi three days ago, have them close some accounts, send money overseas. Fucking idiot..."

Hands stretched out to her sides, she approached Tommy slowly. "It's going to be okay," she said. "We didn't know. You didn't know. What Reverend...what Shaw did was evil. He tricked us." She motioned at the bodies splayed around the pavilion. "All of us."

Tommy bared his teeth, a whine cutting through them. "I...believed."

"We all did. It's okay."

"He..."

She took another step forward. His voice barely rose above the thunder of her pulse in her ears. A part of her didn't know why she cared if Tommy killed her. She'd already lost so much. What was her life compared to the rest?

When she thought about Reverend Shaw commanding them all to lay down their lives, she knew her answer.

"He was a con artist, Tommy. A good one. Look how many people he fooled."

Suddenly, he slapped his free hand around the pistol grip, steadying the weapon. Elizabeth froze. She kept her arms wide, and her breath stuck in her chest as though frozen. Everything felt cold and electric.

"Tommy—"

"Shut up!" His voice cracked with despair. "He didn't...he..."

"He did. I'm sorry."

Tommy screamed. The sound erupting from his throat sounded more agonized than the screams of the dying congregation. He dropped the gun into the field and clawed at his chest and throat. Falling to his knees, he beat his fist on the ground.

"Goddammit!"

Elizabeth gasped when he reared back and slammed his fist into his cheek. He struck again, knuckles colliding hard with his eye. When he punched himself a third time, she raced forward and hooked his arm in both of hers. She feared he'd reach for the gun again, end both of them and complete Reverend Shaw's plan, but instead he collapsed to the ground.

"I'm sorry," he said. His ragged voice was something between a wail and a whisper.

"It's okay," Elizabeth said. She patted his back and then held him close as he shuddered inside her arms. Her lie didn't hurt so much.

"WHERE ARE YOU GOING?" she asked after they'd finally collected themselves. She sat on one of the pavilion's wooden benches, feeling more exhausted than she thought possible. Tommy stood over her, slinging on a backpack. He held a water bottle and stared toward the compound's edge.

"Port Savoi," he said. "We still have people there, if Shaw didn't radio them before setting us off."

"And if he did?"

He turned, running his eyes over the bodies. They were starting to smell in the jungle heat. "Somebody needs to know about this. What happened."

"Right."

"Are you going to come with me? I'm taking one of the trucks."

For a long moment, she considered it. Nothing remained for her in Sunrise Gardens, nothing but the dead. She remembered Carlos, though. He'd done so much, tried so hard, and now he was just another body on the ground. It didn't matter that he'd gone so brutally. She wasn't ready to leave him.

"I'll stay. I need to go looking for Reggie. And I want to bury Carlos."

"Right." He stared into the distance for a long time, breathing angrily. "I'm not coming back."

"Oh?"

"There's…" Again, he looked around. Maybe he was taking in the scene one last time. "This has to go behind me. I have a lot to put back there."

"I get it. What do you think you'll do?"

A shrug moved his shoulders. "I don't know yet. I…maybe I'll just end it."

She searched for the right words, only found, "There are worse things."

"Right." He stood in silence a long time. Even the jungle remained quiet. "So, there are keys in all the trucks, food in the mess."

"I know. I'll be okay."

"You sure? Maybe you should go inside somewhere. It's really starting to smell."

She held back the glare she wanted to give him. Only twenty minutes before, he'd held a gun on her. "Yeah. I'm fine."

"Okay," he said. "Elizabeth, I'm sorry."

"Me too."

"Right."

And then he left. She refused to watch him step past the field of bodies. Instead, she buried her face in her hands and tried not to cry. Even the sound of a truck's engine sputtering to life and then retreating into the distance failed to rouse her.

She needed to look for Reggie, but for now she'd just sit. That was enough. With her eyes closed, she'd sit, and she'd wait until she felt ready to move again.

In her mind, Carlos smiled at her. He held her hand and whispered how much he loved her. They married and started a family. Together, they spent the rest of their days in the utopia of Sunrise Gardens. They were happy.

Exhaustion came. Time unspooled. Seconds became minutes, minutes became an hour.

Something moved. A whisper in the tall grass, like air rasping through dry paper.

Elizabeth looked up. A figure stepped clear of the jungle. Small. A boy.

"Reggie?"

The figure approached with clumsy, lurching steps. She recognized the child's outfit. After hiding, he must have decided to return to the Gardens, maybe search for his aunt.

"Reggie, are you okay?"

He didn't answer, just kept walking, his gait somehow steady and spastic. Could he have broken his leg?

"Wait there! I'll come to you!"

Elizabeth climbed off the picnic table and started across the field. Reggie didn't stop, didn't even slow. He didn't speak. Or wave. He just lurched toward her. Even from such a distance, she saw blood on the boy's clothes. Not a lot, but enough to be visible.

The murmur of droning flies grew. Sunrise Gardens had begun to smell.

She had to make sure Reggie was okay.

What if he wasn't?

Elizabeth kept walking. She had faith.

HORROR DNA

MOVIES
COMIC BOOKS
MUSIC
BOOKS
VIDEO GAMES

IT'S IN
OUR
BLOOD
horrordna.com